BAD DAY AT AGUA CALIENTE

The Department of Justice wanted Yancey Blantine badly! The killer and his renegade crew had wiped out a town and slaughtered everyone in it, before running for the shelter of Mexico. The Attorney-General gave the order to follow Blantine's trail and bring him in alive. He knew one man who could do it — Frank Angel — but he also knew what trouble Angel would face. Meanwhile, through the wild and empty land, the Blantines put out the word . . . kill Angel!

DANIEL ROCKFERN

BAD DAY AT AGUA CALIENTE

Complete and Unabridged

LINFORD
Leicester

First published in Great Britain in 2006 by
Robert Hale Limited, London
Originally published in paperback as
Kill Angel! by Frederick H. Christian

First Linford Edition
published 2007
by arrangement with
Robert Hale Limited, London

British Library CIP Data

Rockfern, Daniel
   Bad day at Agua Caliente.—Large print ed.—
Linford western library
1. Outlaws–Fiction 2. Western stories
3. Large type books
I. Title II. Christian, Frederick H.,
1931 – . Kill Angel!
823.9'14 [F]

ISBN 978–1–84617–854–2

Published by
F. A. Thorpe (Publishing)
Anstey, Leicestershire

Set by Words & Graphics Ltd.
Anstey, Leicestershire
Printed and bound in Great Britain by
T. J. International Ltd., Padstow, Cornwall

This book is printed on acid-free paper

A Note to the Reader

In Record Group 60 of the National Archives in Washington DC, there is abundant documentary evidence to the effect that for a number of years the Department of Justice employed a Special Investigator named Frank Angel, who was directly responsible to the Attorney-General of the United States. There is no record that any of the events in this book took place, or that Frank Angel took part in them. Equally, there is no record that he did not.

1

'No man takes my gun,' hissed the man at the bar, sibilantly. Gould shook his head. No matter how many times you proved it, there was always another one who had to learn the hard way. He let the thought come and go without letting it arouse any emotion. This kind didn't anger him any more, or disgust him the way they once had. He was all over that now.

'Reconsider it,' was all he said. There was no threat in his voice, nothing. He made it sound like advice. If anything, he sounded tired, but there wasn't a man in the saloon who misread his nonchalant stance. Many of them had seen Gould in action and knew exactly how deceiving it was. The city fathers of the border hell that was Stockwood had chosen well when they had picked Dick Gould for their town marshal.

The man at the bar was a thin, stoop-shouldered man of about thirty. Above a receding stubbled jaw, a hooked and aquiline nose jutted over lips drawn tight in a grimace of anger and unholy anticipation. The eyes were deepset and beady as the eyes of a rattler. It was a weak face, the face of a man who has never had to make many decisions for himself. But he had to make one now and those watching saw the touch of indecision alter the outline of his eyes.

'You know who I am?' the man at the bar said.

'It don't matter all that much,' Gould said, laconically. Nobody moved. They had all stood frozen when the beady-eyed one had shot down an unarmed man who had jostled his elbow when he was drinking a schooner of beer. The killing had been shocking, brutally unexpected and the saloon had gone stone silent until Dick Gould came in through the batwings at a half run, to where the weak-faced one had been standing in a well-cleared space in the centre of the floor, a half circle of bystanders watching open-mouthed; wide-eyed, awaiting the denouément, hoping they were out of the line of possible fire. Like people at a circus, waiting for something to happen, waiting for the tightrope walker to fall. Gould could hear their thick breathing.

'I'm Rufe Blantine,' hissed the man facing Gould. 'An' I say again: no man takes my gun.'

There was a total stillness in the place that could almost be felt. Not a man there had not heard of the Blantines. They were a cut-throat crew, every one of the brood spawned by the mad old man whose renegade gang bowed to no law save their own, and whose plundering raids from their mountain hideout south of the Rio Bravo had made them as feared as the warring Apaches. Even here in Stockwood, men would normally walk wide of the Blantines. But if Dick Gould allowed any man to flout the iron hold he had upon his town, he would be laughed out of it by every bum on the border. No exceptions, he had always said. Now he had to make it stick against one of the most feared names south of the San Agustin and Stockwood waited with baited breath to see if he could.

'Last time, Blantine,' Gould said, making his choice. 'Shuck it or use it.'

'Damn yore eyes!' screeched Blantine.

His hand flashed down to the butt of the eagle-bill Colt's .38 in the fancy, tooled-leather holster. He was quite sure of himself and the gun was up and out before he realized that Gould had beaten him. He had just one tenth of a second to assimilate the fact that he was going to die before Gould's bullet smashed into his body and he was dead even as his thin frame was hurled backwards against the bar and slid lifeless to the dirt-packed floor. A thick gobbet of blood bubbled out of his nostrils and mouth and the surprised fear faded as the snake's eyes glazed.

Gould stepped forward. The sixgun was cocked again and ready for trouble. The man was wound up tight like a coiled spring and no one spoke for fear of releasing the terrible killing willingness in him.

'Anyone else?' Gould rasped. There was emptiness in his eyes. 'Anyone?'

'Easy, now, Marshal,' someone murmured. 'He's a goner, sure.'

Gould stood poised for a moment longer, then blinked, the way a man will coming out of a darkened room into bright sunlight. He drew in a long breath and let it out, holstering the sixgun as he did so. He knelt beside the fallen man, checking for signs of life.

'Damned fool,' he muttered, rising. He looked around at the circle of faces craning to see everything. A murmur of conversation had started up. The muscles at the corners of Gould's mouth flickered slightly. He brusquely detailed two of the onlookers to carry the dead man across the street to Doc

Tannenbaum's office, then shouldered roughly through the crowd, past the ones who wanted to touch him, to slap his back or shake his hand as if some special current would pass from him to them, as if he carried some talisman which would bring them good fortune. He had observed the phenomenon many times before but tonight for some reason it made him feel repelled. He needed air, and he got out of there as his deputy, Oscar Thistle, came on up the street, a shotgun ported ready in his stubby hands.

'It's OK,' he said. 'It's OK.' Thistle looked disappointed.

'Awwww,' was all he said. He had seen the look in Gould's eyes, and knew it for what it was. Oscar had been a lawman all his life.

He followed Gould back along the street to their office and went into the building. He did not comment upon the way the marshal had walked blindly through the Saturday night crowd, unseeing, uncaring about the resentful looks he had gotten from those he jostled.

'I need a drink,' Oscar said loudly. Gould was sitting in his bentwood office chair, staring at nothing. The deputy made a lot of fuss about getting the tequila bottle and some glasses out of a cupboard and sloshed some of the fiery liquid into them. He was a short, thickset man of about fifty, dependable, a good backup man upon whom Gould could always rely and knew it. Oscar had bossed a few towns himself in his younger days, until someone had emptied a shot-gun into his back one night as he was playing pool in the back room of a saloon in Fort Griffin. He had pulled through and he had gone after the men who had done it and killed them, but Oscar could never straddle a horse again, never run anywhere, and experience very few days when he did not have any pain. He was getting bald now too and thicker around the middle, but he was still a good man with a gun and it was a long

long time since anyone had made a joke about his name.

'Those goddamned gawkers,' Gould said finally, acid etching his tone. He drank down the tequila in one gulp and pushed the glass forward for more. 'They don't care who the shit gets killed — as long as somebody does.'

'Shore, son,' Oscar said, mildly. 'Human nature, ain't it? Edge o' the precipice an' all that.' He filled the glass and pushed it back.

'You old bastard,' Gould said. 'You're buttering me up.'

'Who, me?' Thistle managed to look astonished. 'Why'd I want to do that?'

'Dammiflknow, old timer,' Gould said, a rueful note in his voice. 'I reckon I might just have pulled the plug out o' the sky tonight.'

Thistle looked up sharply. He had never heard anything remotely like apprehension in Dick Gould's voice before. His eyes narrowed.

'What the hell happened?' he asked, tersely.

'That man I killed. It was Rufe Blantine.'

'Christ 'a' mercy!' ejaculated Thistle involuntarily. Then, seeing the edginess come back into Gould's eye he moderated his surprise and asked non-committally: 'He give you any alternative?'

Gould shook his head. He looked at the tequila bottle for a moment and then, as if coming to a decision, poured himself another drink.

'Rufe Blantine,' he said. He raised the glass ironically.

Oscar Thistle got a plug of tobacco out of his vest pocket and sliced off a chew. He let it get good and settled in his jaw before he spoke again. 'Ain't no way to make yourself popular,' he eventually observed. Gould's face split into a grin at his deputy's colossal understatement. Then it sobered again.

'I know, dammit,' he said. 'It was fair and square, Oscar. I gave him all the rope I could.'

'Knowin' you, I never thought

nothin' else, son,' the old man replied. 'But from what they tell about Yancey Blantine I doubt he's goin' to reckon that's got much to do with anything.'

Gould nodded again.

'You could . . . drift, mebbe.'

Thistle said it very gently, and swiftly raised his hands palms outward as the younger man swung around, eyes blazing.

'On'y a suggestion, boy,' he went on. 'Don't take offence. It might be smart.'

'Smart!' spat Gould. '*Smart!*'

'Yep. Not heroic, mebbe. But smart.'

'Oscar, will you quit that!' snapped Gould. 'You know I'd never get a job anyplace if I ran out on this thing.'

'Not as no town-tamer, sure,' Thistle agreed. 'So what? Ain't sure I wouldn't ruther be a live anonymous than a dead somebody even so.'

'No,' Gould said. 'This is what I do.'

His jaw was set in a firm line and Thistle had seen that look before. He argued no more.

'It's what I do,' Gould said again, as

if confirming a thought in his own head. He got up and went to the door. Opening it, he looked out on to the busy street. On Saturday, Stockwood was always lively. They could hear some of the girls singing in the cribs down at the south end of the street. A cowboy went by, reeling in the saddle.

'It's my town,' Gould said to no one in particular, then hitched his gunbelt around his lean hips and went out into the boisterous street, heading for Doc Tannenbaum's, a good man doing his job.

2

Stockwood slept.

It lay like a scattered set of child's building blocks on the flat scrubland, south of Tucson, east of Nogales and no damned further from the border than it had to be. To the south the Huachuca Mountains reared eight thousand feet, sharp and ugly against the blazing white vault of the sky. East, west and north lay only the emptiness of the Apache desert.

Stockwood was a kind of unofficial staging post, temporary accommodation for drifters and long riders with a wary eye over their shoulder for the kind of dustclouds a posse might make, tank town for Mexican bandits to buy ammunition and supplies, for rustlers to be separated from some of their plunder, for enlisted men from Fort Huachuca to get laid, for the miners of

Santa Rosa to drink away their money. Stockwood was an unlovely huddle of shacks, dug-outs, adobes, saloons and cribs good for nothing except what you could buy in it or sell in it. It had been a wide-open hell town until Al Davies, who ran the general store and had a sizeable sideline in stolen US Army guns and ammunition, and the owners of the two saloons, Pitt and Kingham, had put their heads together and employed a town tamer. They had told him straight: they wanted the town kept on the rails but not closed down. If Stockwood got religion then they were out of business, so it was all a matter of degree. They wanted just enough law to make it unnecessary for the Territorial Legislature to feel it incumbent upon themselves to send in a real lawman. Private law was best, Davies and his cronies felt. You could reason with private law.

So Stockwood was kept in line: just. Dick Gould was a man who knew instinctively when a firm hand was needed. His reputation helped: there were plenty of men in this part of the world who had seen him or heard of his exploits in Hays and with Oscar Thistle backing him up trouble tended to fizzle out rather than blow up in Stockwood. For themselves, Gould and Thistle had a vaguely formulated notion that one of these days they were going to take all the pay they had saved in Stockwood and buy a spread somewhere up in the Jackson Hole country, where rivers ran all year round and a man could see about three hundred miles of green, green grass in every direction. It was something to hold on to when you had to step into the middle of a fracas that could erupt into the mindless smash of sudden death.

Stockwood was no beauty spot. At dawn, no lights showed at the windows of any of the buildings along its one wide street. Only mangy cats prowled after packrats in the unlovely piles of refuse scattered haphazardly between the larger buildings. Slowly the rising sun touched the half grey sky with pinkening fingers, and a blush of light touched the scarred faces of the Huachucas, turning the black shadows at their base to pools of deepest purple. The thin twitter of wakening birds began in the sage-stippled hills and somewhere a lark began its trilling ascent towards the morning. A big old jackrabbit hitchkicked across the edge of the trail to the south of town as a band of men rode towards Stockwood. They rode on horses darker than the dawn, giantlike in the changing light, silent in the hock deep dust. Eight of them, ten, a dozen, twenty, they sifted up the single street and took up positions clearly preplanned, on porches, behind walls, some even climbing in snakelike silence up on to the flat roofs of the buildings. The first probing rays of the strengthening sun touched metal, glinting on the barrels of carbines, etching highlights on bandoliers of ammunition. No word was spoken. The horses were led silently away from the street and all the men at their posts waited, heads up, as if for a signal.

In the first full light of the morning sun, Yancey Blantine raised his arm and jerked it up and down, the old cavalry signal for 'forward'. Pale in the sunlight, flame flared on torches made of dried reeds as the men along the street methodically and with expressionless faces set fire to the houses and the saloons and the stores and the cribs. They moved about their work in total silence, an eerie and uncanny grimness in their movements. The hesistant flames touched the tinder-dry wood and bit, then flickered as if with joy, biting deep and hungrily into the timbers, dancing and leaping joyfully, spreading like liquid fingers, smoke starting to coil upwards in the still morning air.

Still the silent men went on, setting torches to other parts of already burning buildings, tossing the blazing brands upwards on to the roofs with smooth and deadly precision. Now as the flames really caught the men fell back away from the searing heat, grouping in the centre of the street, others behind and around the sides of buildings, carbines ported, sixguns loosened in their holsters, squinting into the flames which now lanced dancing upwards ten, twenty feet high, hurtling a great black oily cloud of smoke into the uncaring vault of the sky. It was very noisy now in the street. The flames roared as a bright morning breeze touched them, encouraged them to greater efforts; the sudden yells, the screams of alarm which came from inside the houses caused no reaction from the narrow-eyed men in the street except for one, one man alone on horseback whose stallion curvetted anxiously in front of the flickering flames.

'*Fire!*'

The cry was heard, repeated, shouted, screamed, cursed. '*Fire!*'

In the street the waiting men heard the shouts and the screams and the curses impassively. Men yelling in fear, bellowing in pain, screaming in panic, women whimpering in terror, and always, always, the dreaded word, the terrifying enemy '*Fire!*'

People were boiling out of the burning buildings. The saloon was an inferno, flames leaping thirty feet high above its roof.

The man on the black stallion drew his sixgun and cruelly yanked the head of his horse around. He thundered up the street at a flat gallop, his sixgun barking in staccato rhythm. A man standing in the street in his nightshirt watched the rider coming towards him in complete astonishment and the man on the black horse shot him down as if he was a target. A woman ran screaming into the street towards the fallen man and shouted something after the rider but he did not turn for now the men who had started the fires had levered the shells into their carbines and they were firing too, a steady and withering hail of lead that sliced into everything that moved, every man and woman who came out of any of the blazing buildings.

Al Davies came out of the shack in which he slept down at the south end of town and ran up the street, seeing only the fire and hearing the shots. He was shortsighted and did not recognize the men in the street until he was very close to them and then he tried to turn and run but one of them shot him in the back. Davies was smashed flat on his face in the dust of the street and tried to crawl away but the same man carefully aimed his carbine again and this time his bullet blew the back of Davies' head to bloody smithereens. Man after man after man ran into the scything, murderous rain of death in the street. There was nowhere to run. Not a building remained that was not afire, and so the men died helpless, puzzled, astonished, shocked, terrified, defenceless against the granite indifference of the killers in the streets of Stockwood. Dead and half dead littered the smouldering sidewalks and the killers stalked among them, killing anything, anyone who moved, merciless and inhuman, showing not the faintest sign of humanity, of pity or of sorrow.

On and on and on the killing went, into the morning. Over the pit of virulent hell that had been Stockwood a huge pall of smoke hung like a waiting shroud as the executioners went about their work, eyes lit by the dying red flames, the barrels of their guns hot from their ceaseless killing work.

Then, at one point, perhaps twenty minutes, perhaps more after the first terrible hail of lead had scythed down the first victims, a terrible yell of triumph went up from the killers, and they dragged before their leader the battered, half-conscious bodies of two men.

They had grabbed Gould and Thistle as they came out of their office into the satanic light of that terrible morning. Thistle had been felled by a smashing blow from the stock of a Winchester carbine, but Dick Gould was not let off so lightly. Him they had neatly ambushed, one to each side of the door, big men, specially chosen for this task. They had smashed him down, picked him up, smashed him into each other's arms, then again and again and again and again, punishing his brittle face bones with hands as big as hams, smashing and grinding and cutting the defenceless man. Then when he was crawling in broken agony on the ground they had used their boots on him, and the wicked spikes of their Mexican rowels, raking the body of the screaming marshal, raising welts of flesh which spurted bright red blood into the unheeding dust.

Just before the point at which they would have killed him they stopped, and one of them brought a bucket of water and threw it over Gould. Then they dragged him in front of the man on the black stallion.

Gould fell on his knees. He could not stand, and only vaguely see. He looked up. The sun was right behind the head of the man on the horse. He looked immense. The bright light lanced into Gould's eyes and he wept unashamedly.

'What . . . what in the name of God . . . ?' he managed, brokenly.

'You use the name of God, you vile animal?' screamed the man on the horse. 'Whoso sheddeth man's blood, by man shall his blood be shed!'

Gould shook his head, pawing the dirt and blood and tears from his eyes. He looked up again. The man on horseback was a huge man, sixty or more years of age. His great bristling eyebrows jutted out over deepset and burning eyes, eyes that burned with a great inner fire, a madness of conviction that nothing but death would shake.

'Blantine?' Gould said.

'I am he,' the man shouted. 'I am he whose eldest son you murdered!'

'But this . . . ' Gould turned his head towards the blazing town. 'This?'

'Aye, this!' screamed Blantine. 'This sink of pestilence, this pile of ordure

— I will destroy it. This place will stand in death as my son's monument!'

'You're crazy!' Gould shouted. 'Crazy! You can't — '

Blantine had a heavy quirt dangling from his wrist. The short whip had a lead-loaded stock. He hit Gould in the mouth with it. The marshal reeled backwards, the lower part of his face a sudden mask of bright blood. Blantine whirled his stallion around.

'Finish it!' he screamed. 'Burn it! Burn everything! Every stick and stone of it! Leave nothing standing! Nothing, you hear me?'

His executioners licked their lips and went about their deadly work. They moved among the ruins and put to the gun anything that moved. Now and then there would be a shout as someone found a woman whimpering in hiding behind a broken wall, down a makeshift cellar. The killers did what they wanted with the women before they killed them. Someone somewhere found some cans of kerosene and they threw the volatile liquid into the smouldering ruins, yelling with coarse delight as the black oily flames leaped high again, roaring upwards. Then they gathered grimly around Yancey Blantine and watched as the old man put Gould very slowly to death.

3

A tall girl with honey coloured hair walked down the corridor of the huge building on Pennsylvania Avenue which housed the Department of Justice. She was a pretty girl with a wide mouth always ready to smile, and impish blue eyes that danced now with awareness of the man who followed her. Annabel Rowe knew Frank Angel was watching her walk, savouring it. And she was pleased in a perverse sort of way. Her whole education and upbringing told her that her thoughts were unladylike and if anything rather forward, yet she found that somehow her hips, as though controlled by some other force than her own brain, swung perhaps just that little bit more than they really needed to do.

Frank Angel watched the intricate movement with appreciation. There was something beautiful about the mechanism of the female pelvis and the Attorney-General's private personal secretary had a beautiful walk. He thought he would like to walk in the mountains with her one day.

She stopped in the antechamber outside the Attorney-General's office and looked at Angel over her shoulder. He was a big man, rangy and wide shouldered. Miss Rowe was a great one for noticing hands, and Frank Angel's hands fascinated her. They were long-fingered and tapered, the hands of a skilled artisan, a musician. She repressed a delicious shudder at the thought that they were also the hands of a killer, for she knew too that Angel, as a Special Investigator for the Department, was a man whose assignments for the Department sometimes — often — required him to kill in its service.

'He's expecting you,' she told Angel.

'Ma'am,' Angel said. Damn him, she thought. Ma'am, indeed. Anyone would think I was ninety.

'I'll see you later,' she said conspiratorially, and then blushed at what she had said.

'Sure would be nice,' Angel told her.

One of the two armed Marines guarding the doors to the Attorney-General's office opened it with stiff military precision and Angel went in. The Attorney-General came forward to meet him, a smile on his face. 'Frank,' he said warmly. 'Come in, come in.'

Angel took his accustomed chair across the desk from the Attorney-General, hastily shaking his head when the Attorney-General lifted the lid of his cigar box and raised his eyebrows.

'Don't know what you're missing,' the older man said, lighting one of the evil black cigars with relish, puffing delightedly on it and exhaling huge clouds of smoke towards the open windows.

'Now,' the Attorney-General said. 'You've read Colonel Kramer's report?'

Angel nodded.

'A patrol from Fort Huachuca got to

Stockwood on the second morning after the raid,' he said, quoting the report he had spent most of the preceding night studying in his apartment. 'They found all the buildings destroyed, livestock stolen or driven off, and forty seven dead among the ruins, eight of them women from the cribs. Several of the women had been the victims of multiple rape. One man had been subjected to torture: a branding iron, the report suggested. From identification found on the body they surmised he was Richard Gould, the town marshal. They couldn't understand the reason for the torture until one of the Apache scouts found tracks going away from the town not made by the raiders. They sent out a search party and found an old man named Thistle all but dead in a runoff about five miles south of Stockwood. He had been shot four times by the raiders, twice through the lung and once through the lower stomach. The other bullet had shattered one of his knees. The old man had strapped a board to his leg with his belt and crawled nearly five miles across the desert, and he died the night after they got him back to Fort Huachuca.'

'But not before he had identified the raiders as the Blantine gang,' the Attorney-General said. 'That scum!'

'Yes, I read the transcript of what he said. That Colonel Kramer out at Huachuca is a smart soldier. Having someone take a stenograph copy of Thistle's story has at least given us some motive for what the Blantines did.'

'The marshal killed one of the old man's sons,' the Attorney-General said, 'yes, I know, I read it too. But to put a town to the torch and kill fifty people — what kind of barbarism is that?'

'Well, sir, from what I've been able to get out of our files on the Blantines, the old man has been a thorn in the side of both the military and the civil authorities on the border for years. He's a law unto himself. He owns that country down there. Nobody can cross it without his say-so. Nobody can get into it without he knows about it. And United States law doesn't reach across the Rio Grande. He's pretty much fireproof.'

'I hope you don't mean that literally, Frank,' the Attorney-General said, relighting his cigar which had gone out again. They always did, Angel reflected. 'Because I' — puff — 'want you' — puff — 'to bring Yancey Blantine in' — puff — 'for trial.'

'Oh, is that all?' Angel said.

'That's all,' the Attorney-General said. 'Any questions?'

'Well, I could probably think of a couple of hundred off hand,' Angel said, a faint smile touching his lips. 'But I get the feeling the answer to every one of them would be the same.'

The Attorney-General smiled, nodding beneficently like a Buddha. He said nothing.

'When do you want me to start?' Angel asked.

'Anything wrong with today?'

Angel hesitated for a moment.

'Well, man?'

'I had a sort of — engagement in mind tonight,' Angel said.

'Break it,' was the decisive reply. 'I want you on your way, and the sooner the better. Frank, I want that old renegade and I want him so badly I can almost taste it. I want him brought out of those mountains and down to Tucson and then I am going to try him in full view of the entire Territory of Arizona for what he did in Stockwood. It will give me a very great personal satisfaction to see that . . . that animal tried and convicted and hanged, and I don't want to waste any time getting at it. So — ' he stood up, extended his hand. 'Good luck, my boy.'

'Thank you, sir,' Angel said. 'I may need it.'

'Very likely,' the Attorney-General said and if he was smiling, Angel couldn't see it.

4

Angel went first to Abilene.

It was quieter these days; the booming cattle trade had used up all Abilene could offer and was now having headier times down the line at Dodge. He got a room at the Drover's Cottage and when he had cleaned up and eaten walked along the tracks until he came to an unassuming building with a wooden sign outside that said, simply 'Vaughan — Guns'. He pushed the door open and went into the gloomy interior. It smelled of metal and oil and he could hear someone hammering in a room at the back. He rapped on the counter and a man came out. He was tall and slim and fair haired, with pale blue eyes and a mischievous mouth. He looked at his customer and his jaw dropped.

'Frank?' he said. 'Frank?'

'Hello, Chris,' Angel said. 'How are you?'

'Well, Hell's teeth, Frank,' Chris said, 'it's damned good to see you! What are you doing in Abilene?'

'Looking for you,' Angel told him.

'Well, Hell's teeth,' Chris said again. 'Listen, let me get my coat. We got to have a drink on this. We'll go over to the Alamo. Wait, now, wait a minute.' He went into the back room and came out with his jacket, struggling to get his arms in the sleeves.

They walked up the street to the big saloon and went into the cool interior, ordering beer.

'How've you been, anyway, you old pirate?' Chris asked. 'I haven't seen you since . . . well, when was it anyway?'

'Seventy-two,' Angel reminded him. 'The Fall of '72.'

'That's right,' Chris said. His face went sober. 'How did that all work out, Frank?'

'All right,' Angel said. There was a look on his face that made Chris realize

33

he would answer no more questions. He ordered another pair of beers.

'So you've come to Abilene looking for me,' he said. 'I'm honoured, but what do you want with a small town gunsmith?'

'Come off that, Chris,' Angel said. 'You're as much a gunsmith as I'm Father Christmas.'

'No,' Chris said doggedly, 'I quit all that, Angel. I gave it up. No more of that stuff. Gunsmithing, that's my racket these days.'

'Sure,' Angel said.

'I got a job, I got a house, I got a pretty little girl who brings me butter-milk and honey,' Chris said. 'I gave all that up, Frank.'

'I'm going down into old Mexico, Chris,' Angel said.

'Lovely,' Chris said. 'Have a nice time.'

'I work for the Government now.'

'Doing what?'

'This and that,' Angel said. 'Whatever needs doing.'

'Ahuh,' Chris said, nodding. 'This and that.'

'I want you to come down there with me.'

'My holidays aren't due,' Chris said. 'Until September.'

'I want you to come down there with me.'

'I can't, Frank. I told you. I gave all that up. I never touch a gun any more except to fix it if it's broken.'

'Sure,' Angel said. 'You're the fastest man with a gun I ever saw, Chris. Don't tell me that.'

'Second fastest,' Chris said. 'And was, not am. I gave it up.'

'A gang of renegades attacked a town called Stockwood, in Arizona,' Angel said. 'They burned the place to the ground, killed nearly fifty people. They tortured the town marshal and then killed him, too. I'm going down there to bring their leader in. Name of Blantine.'

'Blantine? Yancey Blantine?'

'You heard of him?'

'Yes, yes, I have. And Satan. And the

Four Horsemen of the Apocalypse. You're out of your tiny Chinese mind, Angel.'

'I'm going.'

'Like I said, have a nice time.'

'I want you with me.'

'Fat chance.'

'I'm going to get Pearly as well.'

'In a pig's ass.'

'I mean it, Chris.'

'I believe you, Angel. You always were hammerheaded. You'll do it, all right. But not with me along.'

'Have another beer,' Angel said. 'And we'll talk about it.'

'I'm not going,' Chris said. 'What are you paying, by the way?'

'Not a lot,' Angel said. 'But let's talk about that too.'

'No,' Chris said. 'I quit gunslinging. I got this girl . . . '

'Buttermilk and honey, I know,' Angel said. 'Two beers, bartender.'

'Which part of Mexico?' Chris said.

5

They found Gates in Daranga, Colorado, and he was in bad trouble. The saloon sprawled across one corner of the dusty square that all four of the town's streets joined, a hip roofed box with a false front that bore the legend 'The Lucky Lady'. Outside the brightly lit building two men lounged by the door, smoking cigarettes as if they had nothing in God's green earth to do but that. They looked half asleep.

Vaughan and Angel pushed into the crowded saloon, feeling the tension in the place. Everyone in there was watching the play at a card table in the centre of the room, brightly lit by a hissing oil lamp that swung overhead, casting heavy shadows on the faces of the four men playing poker.

One of them was dealing as Angel and Vaughan ordered drinks. He was a big man, with a three-day stubble of beard blackening the lower half of his face. His huge paws made the pasteboards look like postage stamps, and Angel calculated that he would probably stand around six foot three and weigh the better part of two hundred pounds. Every few minutes the man would look at his cards and then look up at the other players, his eyes bright with suspicion and greed. His craggy face was shiny with sweat and he kept looking at the pile of money on the table. The two men sitting on his right and left were dressed in ordinary business clothes, and Angel tabbed them as local men caught up in a game which had gotten out of hand, now staying with it because their investment in the pot was such as to make them plunge deeper than they would ever normally do. The fourth man was as big as the first, but where the dealer carried beef this one carried muscle. Black haired, pugnosed and friendly-looking, his Stetson was tipped back on his head and he looked very relaxed. His pile of chips was very big, much bigger than anyone else's.

'That's our boy,' murmured Angel to his companion. 'And in trouble like always.'

For now he recognized the big man with the unshaven face, and the knowledge brought him no pleasure.

'Bob Blanchard,' he told himself, 'and a long way from Oklahoma.'

Vaughan, standing close to his elbow, nodded.

'Seems like I recall he was run out of Indian Territory on account of some difficulties with the Doolin boys.'

'More than likely,' Angel agreed. 'You spotted all of them?'

'I reckon,' Chris said. 'Two at the door. An' that scar-faced *hombre* over by the rear door. He's got a scattergun, by the way.'

'I noticed,' Angel replied. 'What about corpse-face on your left?'

Chris turned easily back to get his drink, surreptitiously checking out the man standing next to him at the bar. An inordinately thin, tall man, with a curiously grey cast to his skin, he looked like a walking cadaver. Neither man failed to notice, however, that he had two holsters, both tied down, or that his lambent eyes were fixed upon the men at the table with a curious, strained intentness.

'Oh, yes,' Chris said, turning back. 'I think so.'

'That's all, then.'

'You mean you were hoping there'd be more?'

Before Angel could reply, there was an interruption. Blanchard slammed his fist down on the table, setting the coins jingling, stopping the faint hum of conversation in the saloon as if it had been cut off with a knife.

'Goddammit!' yelled Blanchard. 'Got you at last, pilgrim!' He threw down his hand, three aces and two tens, reaching forward with hamlike arms to scoop the huge pot towards himself. His eyes were alight with triumph and he looked around at the people standing near the table as though expecting applause.

'Sorry, mister,' Gates said quietly. He turned his own cards over. Four kings and a jack. There was an immense silence as Blanchard took in what Gates had said, then let his popping eyes settle on the cards Gates had splayed in front of him. Gates himself sat impassive, his hands resting flat on the table.

A strange light flickered in Blanchard's eyes. He looked to right and then to left and although those watching saw no signal, both Angel and Vaughan knew he had tipped the wink to his two *compadres*, the one by the rear door and the cadaverous one at the bar.

'You got the luck, mister,' Blanchard rumbled.

'Seems like,' Gates agreed. 'Another hand?'

'I reckon not,' Blanchard said. 'Seems to me like these cards is a mite too educated for my taste.'

'Meaning?' Gates' voice had gone

suddenly cold and there was a rapid shuffling of feet as people tried to get out of the line of any possible shooting.

'Aw, nothin' personal, feller,' Blanchard said. 'Lissen, I got a proposition. How's about you an' me cut the cards double or nothin'? I reckon yo're inta me fer about two hundred. What you say?'

'It's your money,' Gates said. 'You want to play sudden-death cards it's fine with me. What'll it be?'

'What yu reckon's on the table, then?' Blanchard asked. If Gates could see the open hatred on Blanchard's face, the sneering insolence in the voice, he gave no sign. His voice was as mild as ever when he replied.

'About five hundred, I'd say.'

'Fine, fine,' Blanchard said. 'Let's cut the cards.'

'Not so fast,' Gates interjected. 'Put your money up first.'

'You'll take my note, o' course?'

'Of course . . . not,' said Gates emphatically. He reached forward to take in the money and as he did so,

Blanchard's hand clamped down on his arm.

'Leave it be, sonny,' he said.

Gates looked up, his eyebrows rising slightly. Then he leaned back in his chair, and held the lapels of his jacket with both hands. He looked at Blanchard hard.

'You don't think I'm going to let you get away with that, do you?' he said quietly.

Blanchard grinned evilly.

'I *know* you are, sonny,' he said. He nodded towards the man at the bar, and the one at the rear door stepped forward. The sound of the twin hammers going back on the shotgun was slick and clear in the silence. Blanchard reached forward to take the money and then he suddenly froze, a curious, almost apoplectic expression freezing his grin into a rictus of astonishment. The cold pressure on his neck could only be one thing: the barrel of a gun. Behind him Angel spoke.

'Tell your friend to ease the hammers

down on that scattergun, Bob,' he said quietly. 'Or I'll blow your head clear into Texas.'

The cadaverous man at the bar started to move forward. He, too, froze in unwilling disbelief as a quiet voice at his ear whispered:

'Forget it.'

He turned to see Chris Vaughan looking at him pleasantly, a slight smile touching his lips. There was nothing friendly about the levelled sixgun in Vaughan's hand, however, and the cadaverous one let his shoulders drop about two inches, easing back his weight on his heels again. His hands moved carefully away from the twin guns and his eyes shuttled from Blanchard to Vaughan to Angel and then back again to Blanchard. Gates had looked up and seen his saviours and a wide grin split his friendly face. He started to pick up the money, stuffing it into his pockets. Angel stepped back away from Blanchard, the gun still ready. Gates came around the table and joined them, and the trio started for the door.

'Don't forget,' said Vaughan, gesturing with his chin towards the door.

'As if I would,' Angel replied.

He walked without haste towards the door and stuck his head out.

'Bob wants you,' he whispered urgently.

One of the two men cursed and both of them turned to hurry in, their hands ready by their guns. Vaughan was waiting for them as they came in.

'Evenin',' he said. He poleaxed one of them and the other whirled, his hand going for the gun just as Angel rapped him neatly behind the ear with the barrel of his sixgun. In that moment, however, Blanchard made his move. With a speed astonishing in one so big, he threw himself backwards, kicking the table forward, making a shield of it.

'Get him, Don!' he yelled.

The cadaverous one with the two guns moved like a snake, his hands stabbing for the sixguns tethered at his hips, and the man at the rear door cut loose simultaneously with the shotgun. The air was filled with the whickering whistle of lead dicing through the space which Angel and Vaughan had occupied seconds before. They were already in action, having dropped to the packed dirt floor, rolling aside from the path of the scything lead. Gates vaulted across another table, ending up neatly with his back to a corner of the room, and almost simultaneously the three men opened fire.

Vaughan's shot took the man with the shotgun very neatly about two inches below the breastbone. Angel's unerring bullets smashed the cadaverous one, Don, back dead against the bar. Gates, whose view of Blanchard was completely unimpeded, drove three bullets into the black-bearded man as he brought his gun into use. Blanchard went down kicking behind the table he had knocked over. The whole thing took about seven seconds.

Smoke drifted slowly across the

saloon. Men began to rise from the floor, from behind furniture, their eyes wide at the terrible carnage. There were five bodies on the floor. They looked at the three men who had wrought this havoc, and watched as Angel, Vaughan and Gates stepped backwards towards the doorway.

'Thank you for a lovely evening,' Gates told the bug-eyed onlookers.

'Sorry we can't stay longer,' Vaughan added. They grinned at each other like schoolkids.

'Let's go,' Angel said.

Five minutes later they thundered out of Daranga, heading south for the New Mexico line.

6

They crossed into Sonora just east of Agua Prieta.

They came down out of the Pedregosas, bearded as bandits, and found a little village where they could get rooms above the cantina. A long-haired, sloe-eyed Mexican girl served them drinks, switching her hips as she walked barefoot to the rough bar, conscious of the stare of the strangers.

'I might get to like Mexico,' Vaughan observed offhandedly, 'if the rest'f it's like this.'

'Good place,' Gates nodded. 'Sleep upstairs, liquor downstairs, chickens in the yard, no worries. Wonder if she's got a big sister?'

'More likely she's got a big brother,' Vaughan said. 'With our luck.'

They went through the ritual with the salt and lemon and drank some of the tequila. Vaughan gasped.

'*Chihuahua*!' he said. 'To think I've been wasting all these years getting rust off of guns with acid and emery cloth.'

They ordered more drinks and Vaughan smiled ingratiatingly at the girl as she brought them.

'Yes,' he said. 'More I think of it, the more I reckon we'd be crazy to go any further. This must be the place.'

'What about the girl who brings you buttermilk and honey?' Angel said.

'Girl?' Vaughan said. 'I don't recall any girl.'

'He's cut his picket pin,' Gates explained. 'He's goin' native.'

'A man could do worse,' Vaughan said.

'Wait till you see her Mama,' Gates said and Vaughan fell silent.

After a moment he looked up at Angel.

'All right,' he said. 'You goin' to tell us now?'

'Good a time as any,' Angel said.

'Tell us the plan, *mi coronel*,' Vaughan said. 'Eet is time.'

Angel told them.

They were silent for a moment and then Gates looked at Vaughan.

'Told you,' he said. Vaughan nodded.

'Had to happen,' he replied.

'Allus knew it would,' Gates grinned. 'He finally snapped.'

'All that fancy Eastern living, maybe,' Vaughan postulated.

'Could be,' Gates said with a rueful look. 'You'd never know by lookin' at him.'

'Nevertheless, Doctor, if he is not put somewhere safe he might run amok at any moment.'

'You're right, of course,' Gates said. 'The rubber-lined room?'

'Yes, yes, and no excitement,' Vaughan added.

'It'll take years,' Gates said.

'Better for the world than that he be allowed to walk around loose,' Vaughan said portentuously.

'Cut it out,' Angel said, smiling. 'It'll work.'

'It'll work all right, *capitano*,' Vaughan said, serious now. 'That's what scares the shit out of me.'

'One thing to have the Blantines kind of happen to you, Frank,' Gates ventured. 'Another bowl o' sucama-growl to actually invite it.'

'Let's get some more of that tonsil paint,' Vaughan said. 'I get the feeling I'm going to need it.'

'You've thought this through,' Gates asked. It wasn't really a question. He knew Angel well enough to know that.

'Yes,' Angel said. 'Yancey Blantine has got to stand trial. Killing him won't do. He has to be seen to be tried, convicted, and hung.'

'I'd rather just sneak up an' kill him then run like hell,' Vaughan said.

'Me, too,' Gates added. 'Them sons o' his could be some unpleasant if they took it into their heads.'

'And they would,' Vaughan said. 'They would.'

'You don't have to do it,' Angel said.

'That's right,' Vaughan nodded. 'That's absolutely right. We don't have to do it.'

'We could just turn around an' go right on back to God's country,' Gates said. 'Forget the whole thing. Live a long, happy, productive life.'

'Right,' Angel said. 'Of course, you wouldn't get a crack at the $5,000 reward, but I guess you don't really need the money anyway.'

'Nope,' Gates said. 'I don't need no money.'

'Me neither,' Vaughan added. 'Pearly an' me could get jobs.'

They looked at each other.

'That's a terrible thing to say to a man,' Gates said.

'Terrible thing to say to a woman, come to that,' Vaughan replied. 'OK, *capitano*. We'll do it. But only because it's for the good of the regiment.'

'O say can you see,' hummed Gates, 'by the dawn's early light.'

'Full military honours if we don't pull through,' Vaughan said.

'And . . . ' Gates mock-choked, 'take . . . care of Betsy and the babies.'

'You're both mad,' Angel grinned.

'You can say that again,' Vaughan told him.

7

They kept to the hills for two days, riding after sundown and through the night, quartering south and west and putting long hard miles between themselves and the border. In the high hills above Agua Caliente they split up. Vaughan grinned when Angel told them to 'stay loose'.

'I'm so loose my knees is knockin',' he told Angel.

'Try and stop them before you get to town,' Angel said. 'Or they'll know it's you.'

'Don't worry, *capitano*,' Gates said. 'Us soldiers of fortune is skeered o' nothin'.'

'Bold as brass,' Vaughan said.

'Steady an' true.'

'Steel for muscle an' tequila for blood,' Vaughan said. 'Ten men like us could ride through the Apache nation.'

'*Con Dios!*' Angel said, slapping the haunch of Vaughan's horse, sending the animal rocketing off down the trail that led south and east towards the *placita* of Agua Caliente. He watched the two of them go, a grin lingering for a while on his tanned face. Then he sobered, and gigged his own horse into action.

Agua Caliente lay in a tight valley where the mountains marched in serried yellow ranks all about it, a good sixty miles south of the border. Like most Mexican towns, it was laid out in the form of an X, a dusty plaza at the centre of the two arms of straggling street, its biggest building a whitened adobe church with a single bell tower in which pigeons nested, *broo-borooing* as Angel walked his horse towards the twin-roofed adobe with the deep-recessed windows that bore a sign which read 'Cantina'. Agua Caliente was only a small town, but it was far enough south of the border to be a haven for the desperadoes who had fled from American law, and he saw many Anglos on the streets. This was the heart of Blantine country. Nothing went on here that they did not know about. For a moment he had misgivings about the sketchy plan he had outlined to his two companions, but he shrugged. There was no other way to smoke Yancey Blantine out of his stronghold. Going after him into the mountains would be even more suicidal than what Angel had in mind. Yet the first step of the plan was hinged upon pure luck. He shrugged.

'For the good of the regiment,' he told himself with a grin, and dismounted outside the livery stable. A man sat on a stool at the entrance, inside the cool shadow of the building, whittling on a green stick with a wicked-looking Bowie knife.

'Howdy,' Angel said.

The man eyed him coldly for a moment, checking him out, noting the cant of the gun on Angel's hip; the quality of his horse, the dust on his clothes.

'Come fur a piece?' the man said.

Angel nodded. 'Like to feed the horse,' he said. 'Leave him a few nights, maybe.'

'Stayin' in town, then?' the man said. He made no move to get up from his stool or take the reins which Angel offered him.

'Nope,' Angel said coldly. 'I was planning on a hike up into the mountains on foot. You in the hostling business or what?'

'Keep your shirt on, mister,' the man said. 'Only askin' a civil question.'

'I come a long way and I'm tired,' Angel said. 'How much for the horse?'

'Twenty pesos a night,' the man said. 'Take it or leave it.'

'Like that, huh?'

'Like that.'

Angel pulled a coin from his pocket and flipped it towards the man who caught it without putting down either the knife or the stick. 'Leave him there,' the hostler said. 'I'll look after him directly.'

'I'd as soon you did it now,' Angel said, levelly.

The man frowned, and then got up slowly. He was tall and well-built and he eyed Angel reflectively for a moment. 'Yo're pushy,' he said. 'For a stranger.'

'You mean it ain't wise?' Angel said. 'You're scarin' me to death.'

'Comin' on tough around here won't pay you no dividends, mister,' the hostler said. 'None at all.'

'I'll write to my mother and tell her,' Angel said. 'In case she ever thinks of paying you a visit.'

'Blantine send for you?' the man said abruptly.

'Who's Blantine?' countered Angel.

'Mister, you don't know the answer to that question, you're in the wrong town,' the man said. 'Might be better if you climb right back on your pony an' keep going.'

'I don't understand it,' Angel said. 'The way everyone makes you feel so welcome in these tinhorn runout towns.

You must see so many tough *hombres*, you think you're one yourself. Listen, friend — I don't think I lost any Blantines, and if I had, I'm not sure I'd go looking out for them. I cut my own trail. You want to cross it, you're never going to have a better chance.'

The hostler looked at Angel again, his eyes crafty and bright.

'All right,' he said. 'All right.'

'*Bueno*,' Angel said and turned away, satisfied that he'd made enough of a scene for the man to be sure, as soon as Angel was out of sight, to pass the word on to whoever it was in town that had the ears of the Blantine boys. It was a calculated move, and he was well aware of the dangers. But he was playing the odds. Likelihood was that they'd send someone in to look him over. That would be enough for him to set his plan into operation. He headed for the cantina and paused for a moment on the ramada to light a cigarette he didn't need, checking the building out. Like most of the other structures in Agua

Caliente it was of adobe, the walls thick and solid to keep the interior cool in the blasting summer heat, and yet keep in the heat when the chill of the desert night fell on the valley. Angel looked about him. Across the street some houses, a store, a long low building that might be some kind of hotel. There were few signs outside the buildings in Mexican towns: they didn't go in for advertising like their *Nort Americano* cousins. Knots of men lounged around the plaza, keeping on the shady side of the buildings or beneath the ubiquitous porches, the ramada roofs that sheltered what passed for sidewalks in Agua Caliente. Women were washing clothes in the stone fountain at the centre of the plaza, gossiping loudly, the smack of the wet clothes against the stone loud in the flat hot sunlight. The spirit of old Mexico was strong here, and yet Angel felt something else: as though everyone in the town were conscious of a presence, of the black power of the Blantines. For this was the Blantines' town and its laws were their laws.

It was cool and dark inside the *cantina*. The dirt floor had been freshly sprinkled with water, giving the place a cool, earthy smell that mingled in Angel's nostrils with tobacco smoke and the faintly oily tang of tequila. The furniture was sturdy and plain, tables and chairs all made to withstand rough handling rather than for any aesthetic beauty. Behind the long plank bar which ran the length of the room Angel was surprised to find an American bartender. He bellied up and ordered a beer, letting his eyes briefly touch the men sitting around at the tables. At this time of day most of the Mexican population was deep in its *siesta*. If Angel saw the faces of his two friends, who were sitting at different tables drinking, his expression gave no indication of it.

'New in town?' the bartender asked.

'Yep,' Angel said. 'Gimme another of those.'

'Sure,' the bartender said. 'But you

pay for the one you had first.'

Angel let his eyebrows rise a fraction.

'House rule,' the bartender explained. 'Don't get hairy about it.'

'Wasn't going to,' Angel replied. 'Just unusual, is all.'

'Two dollars American for the beer,' the bartender said. His voice had no inflexion, friendly or otherwise.

'If that's the price of the beer, how much is the whiskey?' Angel said.

'Same,' was the monosyllabic retort. 'Every drink in the house is two dollars American.'

'Might as well take the whiskey, then,' Angel said. 'At those prices.'

The bartender took his money and poured some whiskey from an anonymous bottle into the shot glass on the bar. Angel reached for his drink and in that same second a shot shattered the glass, splashing whiskey all over his arm. The bartender was out of sight below the bar like a flash. Angel wheeled, his eyes narrowed, to face a man standing at the end of the bar. The door of the saloon moved slightly behind him, he had obviously just come in.

'You're very picky, stranger,' he said. 'Don't like our livery stable, don't like our prices, don't like our beer. Maybe you ought to just keep on going until you find somewhere you do like.'

He was a man of medium height, well built, with something of a gut starting to hang over the belt around his middle. Thirty, thirty-five, was Angel's guess, noting the powerful shoulder muscles and the thick neck. He let his eyes touch the smoking sixgun in the man's left hand briefly, then met the cold gaze. The eyes were a flecked green, and in them Angel could see an unholy anticipation, the ready willingness of a killer to shoot at any sign of a fight. He took a deep breath and then let it out slowly, loudly.

'Hey,' he said. 'Easy, mister.'

'I thought you said he was a hardcase?' the man with the gun said, turning towards the livery stable hostler, who stood behind him just inside the door. 'He don't act so tough now.' He turned to face Angel, letting the hammer back down on the cocked gun.

'What's your name, stranger?'

'Angel.'

'You're kiddin'!' The man guffawed. '*Angel?* Like with wings?'

'That's right,' Angel said. 'Like with wings.'

'Well I'll be a bull's balls!' the man roared. 'I ain't shore you wasn't named right, Angel, I ain't at all shore. Mebbe we ought to make an angel of you right now an' save everyone from havin' to listen to your complaints. What you say, Angel?'

'Can't say I love the idea,' Angel replied. He put an ingratiating smile on his face. 'How about if I was an angel an' bought you a drink instead?'

'We-e-ell,' said the man. 'You have changed your tune, Angel. Ain't he, Georgie?'

'Singin' purtier than a medderlark,' Georgie grinned. 'Like an angel, you might say.'

The man with the gun guffawed at this, and one or two of the onlookers joined in, as if anxious to humour him. The man slapped his thigh with his left hand, and shoved the gun back into its holster.

'Damme if I don't let you buy me a drink afore you leave, Angel,' he said. 'Set 'em up, Jerry.'

The bartender, who had been watching warily, ready at any moment to dive again below the protecting barrier of his bar, set more glasses on the counter. Georgie poured large drinks for himself and his friend.

'Here's to you, Angel,' he said. 'It ain't often I can drink to a man who's yeller clear through.'

He tossed back his drink, and his companion followed suit, slamming the glass down on the counter as he finished. 'Gimme — ' he began.

In that moment a shot rang out shattering the glass an inch from his fingers. He snatched back his hand as though it had touched a red hot stove, whirling with blazing eyes which widened with shock when he saw Angel standing at the bar, leaning nonchalantly on his left elbow, the right hand holding a smoking .45 which menaced Georgie and his friend with indiscriminate friendlessness.

'Should've warned you there are all kinds of angels,' he said, easily. 'I'm the short tempered kind. *Now:*' His voice was suddenly as cold as shifting ice — in some polar sea. 'You with the mouth: what's your name?'

'Go to hell,' snapped the man. 'You're so far out of line you'll never leave town alive.'

'You're tempting me,' Angel told him. 'Dangerous thing to do with an angel — look what happened to Satan. I'll ask you nicely one more time and then I think I'll shoot your ear off. Or try, my hand shaking like this I might just blow your head off by mistake.' He lifted the cocked gun and put a pantomime shake into his hand that made the man along the bar blanch: if that finger tightened, the slug would take his head right off at this range.

'Stop waggin' that damned gun about!' he said harshly, just the faintest shade of fear in his voice.

'Then introduce yourself like a gentleman,' Angel said, levelly. 'I don't have all week.'

'Blantine's the name, Angel. Harry Blantine.'

'Ahah,' Angel said. 'You one of those Blantines Georgie was telling me about?'

'You're damned right he is,' blurted Georgie. 'An' you don't know how much trouble you're in, mister!'

'Story of my life,' Angel said. 'You must think you're pretty big around these parts, Blantine. Maybe someone ought to take you down a few inches.'

'Talk's cheap with a gun in your hand,' sneered Blantine. 'You better put it away an' get the hell out o' this country, my friend. Pullin' that iron's the worst mistake you ever made. All I got to do is yell, an' yo're a dead man.'

'Of course, I could put a bullet in your windpipe,' Angel mused. 'At least you wouldn't yell.' He said it in such a way that Blantine went white. This saturnine newcomer looked very capable of doing exactly what he said. Then Blantine's bluster returned. This was Blantine country. The men watching were waiting to see if he would let the stranger get away with running this bluff. If he did, the Old Man would kick up hell.

'Damn yore eyes!' he snapped. 'I got half a mind — '

'It shows,' Angel said coldly. 'No need to advertise it.'

He ostentatiously holstered his sixgun, and turned to the bartender, who had been watching the proceedings open mouthed. No man had ever faced down a Blantine in Agua Caliente before. No man he had ever heard of would show his supreme contempt of their power by then surrendering his edge on one of them by putting his gun up and giving a Blantine half of an even break. Every one of them was fast with the sixgun and he had seen Harry in action. He stood rooted to the spot with fear and awful anticipation, dreading what he knew must inevitably follow.

'Uh . . . uh?' he said.

'That's right,' Angel said encouragingly. 'Another drink. Blantine there'll pay, seein' it was him spilled the last one I had.'

There was a silence in which anyone present might have counted two, and then Blantine shouted an oath, his hand darting for the sixgun at his side. Angel let him get started, wanting everyone in the place to see it. As Blantine's hand closed on the butt of the sixgun, Angel moved. One moment his hand was negligently hanging at his side, empty. The next moment there was a gun in it, levelled, blasting fire. It was almost too fast for the eye to follow, and considerably faster than Blantine, who was no slouch. Angel's bullet burned through Blantine's left forearm muscles, tearing the flesh open to a depth of about an inch, ripping the tissue like a red hot iron, bringing a scream of purest agony from the man, whose gun clattered to the floor. A greasy sick look came into Blantine's eyes as the shock passed and he felt the first sear of pain, and he doubled up shouting, his knees buckling with the agony of his wound.

Angel watched him dispassionately, watched Georgie hastily rip off his bandanna and roughly bind the wound, which had now drenched the man's shirt with blood. Blantine struggled to his feet, his face a mask of agony and hatred.

'By God, Angel,' he ground out. 'You'll pay for this.'

'Sure,' Angel said. Then to Georgie: 'Get him the hell out of here!'

For a brief moment the hostler's courage returned; as if he knew instinctively that there would be no more shooting, that Angel's command indicated it.

'You're as good as dead, Angel,' he

said. 'The Blantines'll take you apart.'

'You better bring a lot of them if they're all that quality,' Angel said, nodding towards the keening Harry Blantine. 'I've seen puppies with more *cojones*.'

'Big talk, Angel,' gritted Harry Blantine, clutching his arm to his body and rocking it like a little girl rocks a favourite doll. 'Big talk. When we come back lookin' for you, you won't be talkin' so big.'

'Get him out of here,' Angel said to Georgie. 'Get him out of here before I shut him up permanent.' He gestured abruptly with the sixgun and Georgie went pale, retreating a hasty step, his hand held out with the palm forward.

He half dragged Blantine towards the cantina door, Blantine cursing as his steps jarred his wounded arm, causing the pain to surge up in searing waves. He turned at the doorway.

'Sleep well, tinhorn!' he shouted. 'It'll be the last time. Tomorrow we'll be back, and God help you then!'

'Who else would He help except angels?' grinned Angel, coldly. '*Git!*'

Another gesture with the gun made Georgie quickly pull the gesticulating gunman outside the building. The door swung back and clunked solidly against the frame. There was a deep silence in the saloon.

'Now: what about that drink?' Angel said to the bartender.

The bartender poured the drink with a shaking hand that spilled liquor all over the planked bar, gawping at Angel as if, truly, he had just come in through the ceiling clothed in celestial glory with tidings of great comfort and joy.

8

'He *what?*' screamed Yancey Blantine.

Harry Blantine told him again.

'An' — an' you *let* him?' screeched the old man.

'I — I couldn't — '

'Damn your rotten liver!' shouted Yancey Blantine. 'You ought to be lyin' dead in town! If you was a man you'd have died afore lettin' anybody face you down in Agua Caliente!'

'He never gave me no chance, Pa,' Harry essayed, sullenly.

'Chance? Chance? Who's talkin' about chances?' The old renegade was in a towering temper and everyone in the big room at the stone ranch house up in the hills above Agua Caliente knew better than to intervene. Harry must take his medicine. They'd all had to do it at one time or another. Crossing Yancey Blantine was as dangerous as stepping barefoot on a rattlesnake.

'He took Harry unawares, like, Mr Blantine,' the hostler, Georgie, offered.

'Shut your snivelling mouth!' rasped Blantine, rounding on the man, who quailed and stepped backwards to safety some yards out of Yancey Blantine's reach. 'I'll teach this whelp to crawl in front of my town!' He snatched a quirt from the wall and it whistled through the air, lashing across Harry Blantine's shoulders, bringing a shout of pain from him. Again the old man struck and again, as Harry cowered away from him, pursuing his son around the room like some grim old prophet out of the old Testament, purging sins. Finally, he stopped, chest heaving.

'Now,' he said, 'now! Tell me who he is.'

'Angel, Mr Blantine. He said his name was Angel.' This from the hostler.

'Never heerd of him,' the old man snapped.

'Me neither,' said Burke Blantine.

Burke was the youngest of the Blantine brood, a husky six-footer with light curly hair and a deceptively boyish face. Broad shouldered, narrow hipped, a natural athlete and horseman. Burke was a ladies' man but nonetheless as dangerous in combat as a wolverine. He had never met a man who could beat him to the draw.

'Any o' you ever heard the name?' the old man demanded querulously. One by one his sons shook their heads: Harry, snivelling on the floor, rubbing his burning. shoulders with his good hand. Burke, lazily at ease in a wood-and-rawhide chair. Gregg, the dull-witted giant, huge even in this land of tall men, his long arms swinging apelike and loose, his low forehead creased by a deep frown as he tried to follow the rapid shifts in the conversation.

'You others — someone musta heerd o' the man!' snapped Blantine. 'He ain't just been minted to give me trouble.'

'It ain't a name you'd easy forget,'

Dave Ahern said. He was Blantine's straw boss, the leader of the riffraff who were recruited along the border when the Blantines went riding.

'He's right, chief,' chimed in Dave Gilman. 'I never heard o' no long rider with a monicker like that.'

Blantine nodded. If Gilman hadn't heard of him, the man had never operated in this part of the world before. Gilman knew the name and records of every owlhoot in the border country. He was the quartermaster for Blantine's renegade army. Gilman, and his sidekick Gene Johnson, the slow-spoken Minnesotan who stood always silently at Gilman's elbow and rarely if ever spoke, were the men who procured ammunition, traded in stolen guns, bargained for stolen horses and all the other impedimenta the Blantines needed when they mounted their raids.

'Mebbe he's usin' the monicker to throw dust in my eyes,' the old man wheezed. 'Whoever he is, he's trouble as long as he's in Agua Caliente.'

He paced up and down for a few moments, his brow furrowed. He shook his head once or twice, muttering to himself.

'It don't figger,' he said once. 'It don't figger at all.'

They watched him, waiting. No decision would be made that was not made by the Old Man. Few of them actually liked him. That had nothing to do with their fear of him, their innate respect for his mad genius. Yancey Blantine was crazy like a fox, they always said. He would put up an idea that sounded completely mad, and then challenge them to knock it down. The more they tried the more they convinced themselves of the essential rightness of the idea.

Yancey was about sixty now, and the years had bowed his shoulders more but little else about him was changed. The energy and determination were those of a much younger man, who could still outride many of his men, outshoot all of them except Burke. The lines running from the corners of the eagle's beak of a nose were deep, and around the eyes and mouth were furrows put there by years of decisions and power. For over a decade no man had stood against Yancey Blantine and lived. South of Agua Prieta, west of the Baja California, east almost as far as the Chihuahua line, Blantine's word was law and few men that rode the owlhoot trail did not know of it. His pale blue eyes now held that querying, questing look, the look of a man with the answer within his grasp and yet unable to touch it. They were cruel eyes. They had watched many a good man die, many a bad one.

'A lawman!' he said finally.

'What? Here in Agua Caliente? Yo're jokin'!' said Burke.

'I'm tellin' you,' the old man repeated. 'Only thing that fits.'

'If he *is* a lawman — an' I'm not going along with you for a second — he's crazy as a bedbug to come south o' the border in the first place and here

77

in the second place,' Ahern said.

'Crazy like a fox, mebbe?' the old man said.

'Whyfor, Mr Blantine?' Gilman said. 'Why'd any John Law want to stick his neck out this far from home?'

'Me, boy, me,' the old man cackled. 'Don't you know there's a bounty on me? Five thousand dollars? Don't you know that?'

'Hell, Pa,' Burke put in, 'there's bounty on all of us. One or two have even tried to collect it.' He smiled, recalling the buckskin-clad bounty hunter in Magdalena who'd tried to take him. Burke had shot him to pieces, first the right arm, then the left, then the right leg, taking a lot of time over it, enjoying the screams, the man's agony as the bullets cut his writhing body to bits.

'Could be, you know,' Georgie the hostler said. 'Now I come to think of it, he had that John Law smell.'

'Yeah,' Harry said. 'Yeah, that might just be it. Mebbe that's why he set me up like that, to get you to react, Pa.'

'Crazy.' The old man shook his head. 'No sense to it. He'd know we'd ride in and cut him to bits. It still don't make sense.'

'Well, if it's you he wants, Pa,' Burke said, 'that's easy. Let me take the boys in to town. I'll take care of our visiting angel,' he grinned at his own joke, 'an' you don't even need to stir from here. Dave or Gregg here can stay with you. That way you don't even show your nose in town just in case he's got anyone backin' his play.'

The old man shook his head.

'I ain't happy about it,' he said. 'It still don't jib to me.'

'Hell with it, Pa,' Burke said, impatiently. 'He's only one man. Me an' the boys can take care o' him right pronto, be back here in time for supper.'

'Well,' the old man said querulously.

'Come on, Pa,' Burke said.

'Well . . . all right,' the old man replied. 'You could be right at that, boy. After all, that bounty's for my scalp dead or alive. Mebbe he's got some idee o' settin' an ambush in town . . . '

'Somethin' like that,' Burke said. 'What does it matter? Gilman! Get the horses. Gregg, you stay here with Pa. You too, Ahern.'

'I don't need no goddammed army to protect me, you young whelp!' snapped the old man. 'Leave Ahern. He's as good as any of you.' His calculated insult brought an angry flush to his son's face, but Burke let it pass. The old man was always goading him. One day . . . He pushed through the knot of men by the door and led the way outside as old Yancey Blantine grinned evilly to himself.

'Feisty little bastard,' he said affectionately.

Ahern grinned. 'One of these days you'll push him a mite too hard, Mr Blantine,' he said. 'Then the fur'll fly.'

'Won't be mine,' snapped the old man, and went to the window to watch his son lead his men off down the ravine towards Agua Caliente.

9

'This could be tricky,' Chris Vaughan told his companion.

'No!' said Pearly Gates in pantomime disbelief.

The two men were just below the skyline of the bluff overlooking the Blantines' stone ranch house. They had left town before dawn, circling through the hills towards the ranch, always wary for any scout or guard from the Blantine place, but they had seen no one. Throughout the morning they had remained on their perch high in the hills, cursing the merciless sun, their chosen task, and the man who had sent them. Only when Burke Blantine had come stalking out of the house and boiled off down the ravine followed by the Blantine crew did they smile for the first time.

'Looks like *el capitano* was right,'

Gates had observed.

'Never mind that,' Vaughan said testily. 'Can you see inside that damned house?'

Gates screwed the field telescope to his eye and studied the buildings below for a few minutes.

'Can't be sure,' he said. 'But I'd say there was two of them in there.'

'Oh, goody,' Vaughan said sarcastically. 'That's only one each if you're right.'

'I'll take the smallest one,' Gates said.

'My hero,' Vaughan replied.

' 'T'ain't nothing,' Gates said. They eased their way over the rimrock and edged down towards the ranch house, using every scrap of cover they could find. When they got close, Vaughan nodded, and Gates moved away on his belly towards the back of the house. Then Vaughan got up and walked out into the open.

'Hello, the house!' he shouted.

He stood out in the open and hoped that he was far enough away for them to be unable to see the sweat that drenched him. Yancey Blantine might just as easily poke a gun out of the window and shoot him down without a qualm. He was playing on the old man's curiosity and he hoped to God he was doing the right thing.

'Hello, the house!' he shouted again.

He saw the curtain move, and then a rifle barrel poked out of the window.

'Who are you?' someone called.

'Name's Vaughan,' he shouted back. 'I'm afoot. Horse throwed me back a mile or two. I need another.'

'Shuck your gun!' came the command. Vaughan ostentatiously unbuckled his gunbelt and let the weapon fall with a dull thud to the earth.

'Step forward!' the disembodied voice told him. 'Keep comin' till I tell you to stop!'

He did as he was told, walking easily towards the house, his hands held away from his sides, the sweat coursing down his face.

'Come out, damn you,' he muttered

under his breath. 'Come out!'

The rifle barrel remained trained on him as he walked forward and then he saw the door open. A thickset dark haired man came into the sunlight, a Winchester carbine ported ready at his hip. Not Blantine, Vaughan thought.

'Howdy,' he said in what he hoped was a friendly voice. 'Can you help me out?'

'Step up here, mister,' the man said, emphasising the command with a gesture from the carbine. 'Let me take a look at you.' Chris Vaughan came up to within about six feet of the man, who made another gesture with the gun that said *stop*. Vaughan halted.

'I ain't seen you afore,' the man said.

'Hardly likely,' Vaughan told him, smiling ingratiatingly. 'I'm on my way to Agua Prieta. Just came up from Caborca. Been working down there on an irrigation project for the Mex gov'ment. On my way home. Damfool horse shied at somethin' an' throwed me. Been afoot for most o' the day.'

The man with the gun looked at him. Vaughan was dusty and sweaty enough to be telling the truth.

'This ain't no livery stable,' the man said.

'Hell, I know that,' Vaughan said. 'I'll pay you for the horse.'

'Where you say you're from, boy?'

Yancey Blantine came to the door. Like the thickset man, he was carrying a carbine. Vaughan noted that the hammer was eared back. He felt sweat trickle down his spine.

'Listen, if you won't let me have a horse, how about a drink o' water?' he said. 'I'm dry as a prayer-meetin'.'

'Give him a drink, Dave,' the old man said. 'Come into the house, stranger.'

There was a bright light in his eye and Vaughan didn't like it, but he came forward. He had no option. Both of the carbines were ready for action and there wasn't a scrap of cover in the open space before the house. Where in the sweet name of Jesus was Gates?

As if in answer to his question, Gates

came up behind Blantine. He had let himself noiselessly into the house from the rear, where he had discarded his boots, and come through the cluttered living-room on stockinged feet.

'Let the guns down gently, boys,' he said behind the two men. Blantine whirled around, the rifle rising as he did, but then he saw the levelled sixgun in Gates' hand, and his shoulders slumped slightly. He uncocked the gun without a word and set it standing against the doorpost. The one he had called Dave looked from Gates to Vaughan in frustrated fury, his jaw muscles bunching.

'Wouldn't make sense,' Gates told him. 'Put it down.'

The old man nodded at Ahern, as though giving an order. Ahern let the hammer down on his rifle and leaned it next to the old man's. Vaughan let his breath come out in a long low sigh.

'Who are ye?' the old man said, venom in his voice and a brilliant light of hatred flickering in the pale blue eyes.

'Nobody you'd know,' Vaughan told him. 'Rope, rope, where's a rope?' he muttered, rummaging around the dusty, untidy room. Saddles, bridles and bits, worn out boots, card-board boxes lay where they had first been carelessly tossed. The floor was gritty underfoot with drifted sand and unswept dirt. It had been many years since Yancey Blantine had brought his wife Betsy up here to live. After her death, no one had ever bothered much about the look of the place. The curtains of which Betsy Blantine had once been so proud were now solid with grime and trapped dead moths. Yancey Blantine never saw any of it. This was his lair, the place he laid his head. The thought of comfort never crossed his mind.

Vaughan found a braided *reata* in a corner, and proceeded to expertly truss up the black-visaged Ahern. He bound the man with what used to be known as a 'Chink's knot', that vicious killer binding that choked a man to death if he struggled to free himself from it.

When he was finished, he looked down at Ahern.

'Let me warn you,' he said. 'That noose around your neck is a slipknot. It's tied to your ankles and around your arms in such a way that if you kick and struggle to get loose, you'll strangle yourself. You understand?'

Ahern cursed, and tried to spit at Vaughan, who stepped back quickly.

The bound man tried to lunge at Vaughan's ankles with his feet, and his blundering movement brought the ropes up tight at his throat, cutting off his wind and making his eyes bulge in their sockets. Ahern gasped and choked for breath and Vaughan stepped quickly in and loosened the knot slightly.

'Naughty boy,' he said, wagging a finger like an elderly schoolmarm.

'Who are ye?' Blantine asked again. His eyes darted from Gates to Vaughan and back constantly, as if trying to place them. 'Who are ye?'

'We're sort of doctors,' Vaughan said. 'We heard you were ill, so we came up here to recommend a trip.'

'For your health,' Gates grinned.

'A change of air,' Vaughan added. 'Do you good.'

The old man nodded, his eyes sharp and birdlike.

'That Angel feller,' he said. 'Now you.'

'What Angel feller?' Vaughan asked innocently. 'You seeing angels, old man? You do need a change of air. Next thing it'll be pink elephants.'

'Usually is,' Gates said. 'Classic symptom.'

'Ye damned fools!' the old man spat. 'Think ye can get away with somethin' as stupid as this? My boys'll run you down within a few hours.'

'Noisy in here isn't it?' Vaughan said.

'All that chatter,' Gates told him. 'Gives you a headache.'

'Still, he's sick, poor old soul,' Vaughan said.

'We'll humour him,' Gates decided. 'Go get the horses.'

Vaughan nodded and went out. The

old man looked at Gates and then looked at the two carbines by the door. Gates grinned.

'You'd never make it,' he said.

'Think I'm an idjut?' the old man snarled. 'I ain't.'

'I heard that,' Gates admitted.

'You look a smart feller,' Blantine offered.

'Mother allus told me I was, too,' Gates grinned.

'Lissen, man! I'm serious! You can't get me away from here.'

'You a bettin' man?' Gates asked.

'Yep,' the old man said. An evil grin touched his face. 'In fact, I'm willin' to bet you five thousand dollars you can't.'

'How would I collect?'

'Easy, man, easy!' the old man hissed. 'There's money on the place. I could tell you where. Think of it!'

Gates looked at him. He let nothing show on his face. The old man went on, encouraged by Gates' silence.

'All you got to do is get rid o' your sidekick,' he urged. 'Give me my carbine, I'll do it. Then I'll give you the money, an' you'll be free and clear. You can ride out o' here a rich man.'

'Marvellous,' Gates said. 'You sound like you actually mean it.'

'What the hell does that mean?' rasped the old man.

'You oughta go on the stage, Blantine,' Gates said. 'I never seen such good actin'.'

'Damn you for a pigheaded fool!' snapped the old man.

'Aw, you was just sayin' I was such a smart feller, too,' said Gates, wounded pride in his voice. Vaughan came in as he said it, and looked his surprise.

'What was that?'

'Blantine here is miffed on account I won't give him a gun to bushwhack you.'

'Well, thanks,' Vaughan said.

'He offered me $5,000,' Gates told him. 'It was a struggle to say no, I can tell you.'

'Yo're both loco,' the old man snapped. 'Crazy. Who put you up to this, that Angel feller?'

'There he goes again,' Vaughan said. 'His condition's deterioratin'.'

'Better get moving,' Gates said. 'Sooner we can get him out of this unsuitable environment, the quicker he'll get well.'

Vaughan stopped to pat Ahern on the head.

'Don't you go out until yore Daddy comes home, hear?' he grinned.

Gates was binding the old man's hands in front of him, wrists crossed. He was none too gentle and the old man swore once or twice as the rope burned his skin.

'Be a lot worse in Hell, old timer,' grinned Gates. 'Let's ride.'

'I'll dance on yore grave, you — !' spat Blantine.

'But not this mornin',' Gates told him. 'Get aboard!' He heaved Blantine none too gently into the saddle, and swung up into the hurricane deck of his own horse.

'Chris?' he said.

'Ready, *mi coronel!*'

'Why are ye doing this?' wailed the old man, frustration and anger almost making him weep. 'What's behind it all?' Gates looked at Vaughan.

'Shall we tell him?' he said.

Vaughan nodded.

'It's for the good of the regiment,' Gates said.

They jabbed the spurs in and rocketed off down the ravine, swinging sharply left when it opened up on the sage speckled plain, moving off north-easterly towards the long low line of the mountains on the far horizon.

10

Angel was waiting for them in the hills.

When Vaughan and Gates came over the crest of the hill he rose from the shade of the live oak where he had been hunkered down resting and walked into the open where they could see him. They cantered across the open space towards him.

'Havin' a nice vacation?' Gates asked.

'Passable,' Angel grinned. 'How did it go?'

'Fine as snake hair,' Vaughan assured him. 'You?'

'Likewise. I waited until they got into town and then slid out without being seen. I think I got everything we need.'

He gestured with his chin towards the packmule tethered to the tree next to his horse. Then he turned his attention to Yancey Blantine.

'Blantine,' he said. 'My name's Angel.'

'Knew it,' the old man told him. 'What's your game, Angel?'

'I'm taking you to Tucson for trial.' Angel said. 'The United States has got a whole list of reasons for wanting you.'

'Pah!' said Blantine. 'You'll never get to the border.'

'Everyone told us we wouldn't get you out of Agua Caliente,' Gates put in mischievously. 'Look at you now.'

'Bluff,' sneered Blantine. 'You think my boys is goin' to let you get away with runnin' a sandy like this? There ain't a place between here an' Tucson you could lay your heads 'thout my boys hearin' of it. They'll enjoy watchin' you all die.'

'Talk, talk, talk,' sighed Vaughan. 'He never stops, you know that?'

'You'll see, damn your eyes,' raged the old man.

'What now, Frank?' Gates asked.

'We got to cover some ground,' Angel told his companions. 'The old man's right — so far we've played fools for luck, but it can't go on. From here on in, we've got to out-think, out-ride, out-guess the lot of them. It won't be easy.'

'I was afraid of that,' Vaughan said.

'Let's ride,' Gates suggested. 'I keep hearin' hoofbeats.'

'Wash your mouth out with soap,' Vaughan said, 'for saying such a thing!'

They swung the horses around and pointed north and west, as Angel got into the saddle and led the way up again into the sage-dotted hills. There was no trail, no track for them to follow. Angel was heading straight into the malpais, the badlands of mountain and desert that lay ahead of them for a hundred and more miles.

The sun was directly over their heads now, striking down with an almost tangible force, leeching the moisture from the bodies of men and horses, slowing their progress to a walk, and when they were working their way across the pitching slant of treacherous foothills, moving now up and around the huge shoulders of windscoured mesas, their pace became that of an old man walking.

On and on they went across the empty land, antlike against the hugeness of the towering hills, Angel keeping them to where the ground was flinty and hard, where the tracks they were leaving would be hardest to find. Ahead of them stretched the endless vista of tumbling land, scoured across with straggling lines of washes and gullies, dun brown with the scattered ocatillo, prickly pear, and yucca, the mesas grey blue against the horizon, rocky outcrops isolated on the flat brown sea of land like stranded whales. Dust sifted up and coated them, toning down the colouring of their clothes, the textures of their skin, the coats of the horses, to a uniform sandy grey. The horses plodded on.

'I'll kill that Horace Greeley,' Vaughan said.

★　★　★

Burke Blantine led his men into the plaza and pulled his horse back on its haunches in a spectacular stop that caused dust to boil upwards for twenty feet outside the cantina. He shouldered his way past a knot of open-mouthed gawkers by the door and went into the almost empty saloon.

'Where is he?' he shouted. The bartender, Jerry, looked startled.

'Where's who?' he quavered.

'That cheese-faced bastard who shot Harry!' yelled Burke. 'Angel! Where is he?'

'I dun — I dunno, Burke,' the bartender stuttered. 'I ain't seen him.'

A frown touched Blantine's face, the first tentative edges of the knowledge that he had been had coming into his eyes. He rushed outside. 'Search the town!' he yelled to his men. 'Everywhere! Someone must have seen him!'

The men scattered to their task, and Pete Gilman swung down from the saddle and walked across to where Burke Blantine was standing, pounding one fist into the open palm of his other hand.

'He's gone?' Gilman made it a question, but Burke made no answer, for he knew Gilman's thoughts and his own were running parallel.

'I reckon,' he said.

'Aw, well,' Gilman said.

'It's . . . it doesn't smell right,' Burke said tentatively.

'Huh?'

'It all smells wrong,' Burke said. There was a certainty forming in his mind and he knew what it was and he was afraid to utter it in case his hunch was right. Angel. Arriving in town, practically daring the Blantines to come in after him. Why? Then when his challenge had been taken up — and he must have known it would be — he was gone. Again, why? To prove what? Or was it . . . could it have been? No. He wouldn't let himself believe it. Not yet.

'No sign of him,' Gene Johnson said, panting from the unaccustomed exertion afoot. 'Someone said he bought a lot o' stuff at the store.'

'What?' Burke rounded on the man. 'What did you say?'

'He — someone said he bought stuff at the store.'

'Supplies, you mean?'

'I don't know, Burke. One o' the boys — '

'Find out, damn you!' screeched Burke. 'Get at it!'

His men were back around him in a few minutes with the full story, as Burke paced up and down on the ramada of the cantina, up and down and up and down, pounding his gloved fist into the palm of the other hand. Food, yes. He'd bought a packmule. What fool had — never mind. What else? Ammunition. Yes, of course. Blasting powder? What the hell . . . ? Water canteens. How many? Six, someone said. Burke was nodding, nodding.

'What's it all about, Burke?' his brother Harry asked finally.

'I'm . . . I . . . it's just possible,' Burke said. His voice was not much louder than a whisper. Then he snapped upright, his head coming high and the commands lashing out.

'Gilman, Johnson! Take three horses each and kill them if you have to, but get to the ranch and check on the Old Man. If there's anything wrong get back here as fast as you can. And I mean fast!'

They looked at him with startled comprehension dawning on their faces, and without a word swung into the saddle, rocketing off out of the plaza and away up towards the north-west, low in the saddle, straining to get every ounce of speed the horses could give them.

'Harry!' The tone of his brother's voice made Harry Blantine forget his wounded arm. He jumped forward. 'Get going — I want you at Olan Crumm's place tonight!'

'Hell, Burke, that's nigh on fifty miles,' Harry complained.

'Don't you argue with me now!' growled Burke Blantine and there was such violence in there behind the blazing eyes that Harry cringed away from his brother and nodded.

'All right,' he whined. 'All right.'

'Tell Olan to stand by with every man he's got. All the guns an' ammunition he can lay his hands on. He's to be ready to ride before sunup.'

'Sunup,' repeated Harry. 'How will we know?'

'You'll know,' Burke said grimly. 'Get goin'!'

They watched Harry swing awkwardly into the saddle, and even as he was doing so, Burke had turned to his other brother and now his voice altered. He spoke slowly, soothingly.

'Gregg,' he said. 'I want you to do something for me.'

'Sure, Burke,' the giant said cheerfully.

'It's very difficult, Gregg,' Burke told him, and Gregg frowned. He didn't like difficult jobs.

'Do I got to remember anything?' he asked.

'Somethin' real small,' Burked said gently. 'You can do it easy, Gregg.' Gregg swelled with pride at this.

'I want you to ride up to Santa Elizabeta, Gregg,' Blantine said. 'As fast as you can.'

'Sure, Burke,' Gregg said. 'I c'n do that easy.'

'I know you can, Gregg, that's why I'm relying on you. Now: when you get there, go see Dave Hurwitch. You know Dave, don't you?'

'Yeah,' said Gregg eagerly. 'He runs the saloon.'

'That's it. Tell Dave — now this is the important part, Gregg, so try an' concentrate — tell Dave there's a $1,000 reward for the man who brings me Angel.'

'$1,000 reward for the man who brings you Angel,' Gregg repeated. 'Gee, that's easy, Burke. I c'n remember that easy.'

'Good boy,' Burke said. He slapped his brother's massive shoulder. 'Get on that horse an' ride, Gregg.'

Gregg nodded, a huge grin on his face. He swung up on to his horse and larruped it around the withers with the long reins. The startled animal bucked a little, and then Gregg thundered off across the plaza heading due north towards Santa Elizabeta.

'You never sent any description of Angel,' one of his men pointed out. Burke grinned evilly.

'That's right,' he said. 'Dave'll be so anxious to clap his greasy paws on that thousand he won't let any stranger get through Santa Elizabeta until he's absolutely goddammed certain that the man ain't someone called Angel!'

'What now, Burke?' another man called.

'We wait,' Burke Blantine said. 'I could be dead wrong, in which case, no harm's done. All we got to do is catch one yappin' cur. But if he's laid a finger on the Old Man . . . '

He looked up the far hills and his eyes narrowed. The gloved hand curled again into a fist and he smashed it into the flat palm of the other hand.

11

Night found the fugitive quartet in a box canyon which Vaughan had seen up to the north-east, a high walled, narrow crack in the rocky mesa they had been skirting. They eased the horses up to the sloping wall at the closed end of the canyon, and made camp.

'No fire,' Angel said.

Vaughan looked at Gates glumly.

'You bring anything?' he said.

'Un 'hunh,' Gates replied.

'Great,' Vaughan said. 'No coffee, no whiskey. Looks like bein' a chilly night.'

'You can dream of buttermilk and honey,' Angel told him. 'Break out that pack an' we'll eat. I got some cans o' beans in there.'

They hunkered down and ate an unappetizing cold supper. Blantine gestured querulously with his bound hands.

'You ain't gonna keep me tied up like this, are you?' he grumbled. 'I ain't got any feelin' in my hands any more.'

'Things are tough all over,' Angel told him. 'Do the best you can.'

'Goddamn you, I can't eat like this,' fumed Blantine.

'Starve, then,' Gates said coldly. He wolfed down the cold beans as if there was a famine coming. Vaughan watched him with unabashed wonder.

'Look at him,' he said to nobody in particular. He poked at the cold beans on his tin plate with thinly concealed disgust.

'Don't you want them beans?' Gates said.

'I should've stayed in Abilene,' Vaughan replied, handing over the plate. When they had finished eating, Angel told them to get some sleep.

'I'll take first watch,' he said. 'Two hours each. I want to be moving again before sunup.'

'Run all you like, Angel,' Blantine nagged. 'My boys'll catch up with you.'

'Oh, shut up,' snapped Vaughan. He pushed the old man backwards, and Blantine rolled over, lying down perforce. 'Go to sleep before I bend a sixgun over your thick skull.'

Blantine glared at him with undisguised hatred.

'You'll pay,' he hissed. 'You'll all pay.'

'Yack, yack, yack,' Vaughan said, making a quacking gesture with his fingers.

Blantine spat and rolled over, pulling a blanket around his shoulders. He lay on the ground, his eyes unwinking and full of hate. After a long while, the yellow eyes closed and the old man slept, dreaming of revenge.

★   ★   ★

Towards dawn, Gates shook Angel's shoulder. Angel came instantly awake, coming up off the ground with a sixgun in his hand.

'What?' he said, tensely.

'I ain't sure,' Gates whispered. 'Listen.'

The floor of the canyon was in pitch blackness, and Angel could only faintly see the faint tinges of grey on the eastern sky which heralded dawn. Blantine's snores reverberated off the rocky walls.

'Listen,' Gates said again. 'There.'

Angel heard it then. The call of an elf owl, the tiny predator which makes its home in the trunk of the saguaro. Faint, yet clear. The silence was intense again, and both men crouched as still as statues.

'There!' Gates whispered. They heard it again, but this time from the other end of the canyon.

'Two,' Angel said.

'Wait,' Gates whispered. He slithered across to Vaughan's huddled form and touched the sleeping man's shoulder. Vaughan's eyes opened and he started to sit up quickly. Gates pressed him down.

'Easy,' he hissed. 'We got visitors.'

The elf owl *oop-pooped* again. Moments later the reply came. There was a faint increase in the light on the horizon now. Scrub and bushes began to take on recognizable shapes. A turkey gobbled somewhere up on the rim of the canyon and Gates' head came up quickly. He held up three fingers to Angel, who nodded.

'Hey,' Vaughan said.

They could hear each other breathing. The old man snorted in his sleep and Vaughan jumped.

Gates unsheathed a murderous-looking Bowie knife and held it up so Angel could see it. Angel nodded vigorously and showed them his own. Vaughan shrugged. He never carried a knife. His hand strayed to the butt of the gun at his hip. Gates put a finger to his lips and Vaughan rolled his eyes as much as to say, what do you think I'm going to do, scream?

Once more they heard the thin cry of the elf owl, and its echo. They sounded nearer, somewhere on the floor of the canyon.

Angel had moved with infinite care

about ten yards to one side of the campsite. Gates and Vaughan were crouched together six or seven yards away from the recumbent form of Yancey Blantine, who still slept the sleep of the innocent in the open between them.

Vaughan turned to whisper something to Gates and in that instant the Apaches came out of the ground, screaming at the top of their lungs as they launched themselves upon the camp.

★ ★ ★

Burke Blantine led his men up into the foothills of the Santa Eulalia mountains, rendezvousing with the riders from Olan Crumm's ranch an hour before sunup. Olan Crumm was a huge, massively built man with a chest like a barrel, a belly of gargantuan proportions. His treble chins wobbled as his horse fretted in the cool chill of the predawn darkness.

'This is a hell of a thing, Burke,' he said.

'They can't have gone far,' the Blantine son replied tersely. 'We'll catch up on them.'

'Ain't no tellin' whichaway they'll have headed, boy,' Crumm said in his rumbling bass voice. 'They headed for Agua Prieta, they could be someplace up in the Santa Elizabetas, gettin' further away every minnit.'

'That's bad Apache country up there,' Gilman said. 'They get into them hills, they ain't likely to git out in one piece.'

'Hell, they's Injuns all over these mountains,' Ahern said. He was impatient to be on the trail of the men who had so humiliated him. 'My money says they'll be headin' for Nogales.'

'Across the badlands?' Burke queried. 'That's hard ridin'.'

'They ain't likely to use the road, boy,' Olan Crumm rumbled.

'They do an' they're done fer,' Harry Blantine said. 'Nobody can go within

111

ten miles o' Santa Elizabeta without Dave Hurwitch hearin' about it.'

'You covered everythin' pretty good, boy,' Olan Crumm complimented Burke. 'What made you figger they'd try to snatch yore Daddy?'

'Ain't sure,' Burke told the fat man. 'Just this Angel feller, he didn't ring true any whichway you looked at it. On'y when we fell for it I realized he might just be decoyin' us. Too late then, o' course, damn him!'

'So: what do we do?' Ahern asked impatiently.

'We better split up,' Burke said. 'Olan, mebbe you an' some o' your men can check the west side o' the Santa Eulalias. Pete Gilman an' Ahern can see if they's any fresh sign on the Santa Elizabeta side o' the valley. Me an' the rest'll head on into the mountains an' see if we can cut sign there. Anyone finds anythin' send a runner damn fast — I don't care how many hosses we kill, I want them three found!'

'Well, they's enough of us to cover plenty ground,' Crumm said. 'Mebbe we better get started. Be dawn in a little while.' He jerked his chins towards the east, where faint streaks of pink were painting the dark grey underbelly of the sky a lighter shade. They could see the far peaks of the Santa Eulalias blacker against the darkness than the darkness itself.

'Gilman, Ahern, Johnson, you three others head across the valley,' Burke Blantine said, pointing to the west. 'Harry, stay with me. Olan, if you'll let me have three o' your boys, we'll point due north into the — '

He stopped. Far off to the north, he heard something.

His eyes narrowed, and then widened. Olan Crumm looked at him and nodded.

'Gunshots,' Crumm said. 'Sixgun, sounded like.'

They listened again but there was no further sound.

'Couldn't be anyone else,' Ahern

113

said. 'Could it?'

There was a look of wholly triumphant glee on Burke Blantine's face. He raised the quirt and slashed it down on the rump of his horse. The startled animal leaped into a gallop and behind Burke Blantine the fifteen riders streamed in pursuit, heading up into the hills, up to the north, homing in on the sounds of the gunfire that could have only been made by the men they were going to kill.

12

The two Apaches came out of the ground so near to them that Vaughan jumped with surprise, waiting for a moment to drop one of them, the two bucks sprinting across the sandy floor of the canyon weaving and dodging like hunted deer, coming straight at Blantine, who had sat up like a jack-in-the-box at the first scream from the Indians and was watching them as helplessly as a bird watches a cobra.

The first Apache came up level with Angel and launched himself into a flat dive which Angel met with his boot held rigid in front of him, jarring the Apache aside, knocking the man down to the ground. Angel drove in after the fallen Indian but already the warrior was rolling away, incredibly agile, finding his feet again and whipping a wicked curving arm back across his body, the rigidly held knife missing Angel's stomach by inches as Angel swerved to avoid it, coming to a ready position in front of the stinking Apache, the black eyes riveted on him full of the promise of death, both men holding their knives flat on the palm, feinting once twice, then driving in at each other, the Apache howling his courage cry, a cry that turned to an agonized choking gurgle as Angel let him come in and then half turned so that the Apache's knife slid beneath his arm, trapping the thrusting arm and bringing his own knife up in a terrible, ripping, pulling slice that opened the writhing Apache's body from groin to breastbone. Angel felt the hot warmth of the spurting blood and the Apache fell back, all of the breath going out of him in one shocked and enormous gasp, his bulging eyes looking down at the quivering steaming mess of his own insides sliding over his breechclout. Angel hefted the knife quickly in his right hand and hurled it with all his strength. The blade disappeared in the Apache's neck just above his left shoulder blade. He turned his head as though to see it and felt the sharp inner rigidity of the steel slice through everything inside his neck and then he was dead on the floor, his blood soaking the greedy sand.

Gates was still rolling on the floor in desperate combat with the other Apache. Vaughan danced around the boiling dust they were thrashing upwards in their death struggle, trying to get a chance to help his friend, unable to do anything for fear of hitting Gates, who had a vice-like lock with his left hand upon the wrist of the Apache's knife-hand, just as in turn the Indian's hand was locked on Gates' right wrist. They struggled to their feet, Vaughan still dancing around them as Angel came running across the canyon and then Gates picked the Indian up and killed him. It was as awful, as simple, as terrible as that. They saw the huge muscles across Gates' back bulge with a

Herculean effort as he swung the Apache around. The Indian gave a screeching cry of panic as Gates got him up off his feet and then lifted the kicking, writhing, struggling Apache up over his head and then in one swift movement brought the man down across his own bent knee. The terrible dry crack of the man's spine brought a horrifying scream of agony simultaneously from the Apache, who was dead even as his vocal chords made the sound. Gates rolled away from the Apache, then quickly kicked the knife aside. He stood up, swaying, his whole body drenched with sweat from what he had done. He looked at them with blank eyes and they did not move for a moment, and then Vaughan said 'Sh-it!' and started running up towards the end wall of the box canyon.

Yancey Blantine, while they were fighting the Apaches, had scuttled off up the canyon and was trying awkwardly to get at one of the Winchester carbines in the saddle holsters. He was tugging at the butt of the gun with his bound hands when the third Apache came up off the rim of the canyon wall, knife in hand, launching himself into a perfect trajectory to land on top of the old man and plunge the knife into Blantine's unprotected back.

And in that one terrible moment Chris Vaughan's hand flickered to the gun at his side and it came up in a movement too fast for the eyes of any of them to follow. The sixgun blasted once, twice, and the Apache's falling flight seemed to alter slightly as all the rigidity went out of the arched body, and Yancey Blantine threw himself to one side as the body of the Indian hit the ground beside him with a terrible sound, the meaty thwack made by a butcher's axe on a carcass. Vaughan was already by Blantine's side, and he kicked the old man out of his way unceremoniously, his eyes narrowed and the sixgun ready cocked. But the Apache was dead, and Vaughan straightened slowly, letting the hammer down on the sixgun and turning to face Angel and Gates, who came running now up the canyon.

'Nice shootin', Chris,' Gates said.

'But bad timing,' Angel added. 'Not your fault, Chris: there wasn't time for anything else. But in this country — '

'You can hear gunshots for twenty miles,' leered Yancey Blantine. 'My boys'll have heard 'em, sure. They'll be killin' their horses to get over here, Angel! The three o' ye'll be swingin' from a branch afore sundown!'

Chris Vaughan whirled on Blantine and the old man started back in fright at the naked killing lust in Vaughan's eyes. The change from the usually easy going, high bantering man he had so far seen was so complete that Blantine could not speak, and a solid ball of fear clogged his throat as Vaughan angrily eared back the hammer of his sixgun, snarling:

'Damned if I don't kill you anyway, you bastard!'

For one long terrible moment, Yancey

Blantine looked straight into the jaws of Hell. Then Gates spoke, his voice soft and easy.

'Be a shame to blow the reward, Chris,' he said.

Vaughan blinked. Then he blinked again and the fire died in his eyes, to be replaced by a wry, self-amused look. A smile touched the corners of his mouth and he uncocked the gun and slid it back into its holster in a fluid, easy movement.

'One more time, Blantine,' he said, softly. 'Just try it one more time.'

Blantine's bluster returned now that he knew the awful moment was past.

'There won't need to be one more time, sonny,' he cackled. 'You're on your way to Hell right now, an' all I got to do is wait.'

'Get on your horse, Blantine,' Angel snapped. 'Jump!' He emphasized the orders by stepping towards the old man, who recoiled and hastened to get into the saddle. Gates finished saddling the other horses and threw the rest of their gear together hastily, hitching it on to the pack mule with rapid loops of the ropes. Blantine watched him with hooded eyes.

'Let's go!' shouted Angel.

They thundered out of the box canyon into the open, the horses buck-jumping upwards against the sharp slope, the four of them in line astern heading fast and recklessly into the rocky fastnesses of the Santa Eulalia Mountains, moving north, ever northwards.

13

The buzzards led the hunters to the box canyon.

Jud Young, one of Crumm's men, circled around the campsite, squatting every now and again to look at the ground. He turned the Apache whom Gates had killed over with the toe of his boot, and the watching riders heard him give a low whistle.

'Come on, Jud!' snapped Blantine impatiently.

'Easy, son,' Olan Crumm advised. 'Jud's the best tracker 'tween here an' Santa Fe. Ain't no damn use a-tall in apushin' him.'

Young had scouted the whole canyon now. He stopped again by the dead Apache, shaking his head, and then came back to where Blantine and the others waited, their horses tossing their heads impatiently.

'Quite a scrap,' he said. He was a leathery, heavily built man with a wad of chewing tobacco making a bulge in his cheek. His drooping moustache was stained and ragged. Young spat accurately towards the dead Apache, making the clouds of flies humming over the body flurry upwards in a buzzing horde.

'I'd say they was jumped around sunup. Prob'ly a huntin' party. Them Injuns figgered they was in luck findin' three white-eyes all alone out here.' He shook his head. 'I tell you,' he said.

'Come on, man!' Burke Blantine burst out.

'Way I see it,' Young said, shifting the wad of tobacco in his mouth and taking absolutely no notice of Blantine's outburst, 'they come up the canyon at a run, left one man on the rim to work his way round an' take them from the rear. No sign o' blood anywhere away from the Injuns, which means none o' them we're looking for was wounded. But they shore made a mess o' them

Injuns.' He indicated one of the Apaches with a gesture of his chin. 'Someone bruk that buck's back like a stick. That ain't no easy way to kill Injuns.'

'They didn't want to use guns,' Blantine said. 'They knew we'd hear gunfire.'

'Prob'ly had no choice,' Young told him. 'These two here was killed fust — one with a knife, the other like I told you. That 'un over yonder's got two slugs in him. Tried to jump 'em from the rim back up there.'

'Can you tell where they went?' Blantine said.

'Sure,' Young grinned, mounting his horse. 'They left tracks a kid could foller.'

'Which way they headin', Jud?' Crumm asked.

'North, I'd say,' Young replied. 'Prob'ly aimin' to come down out o' the mountains through Apache Pass, east o' Santa Elizabeta. It was me, I'd be headin' for the malpais.'

'The desert?' Ahern queried.

'Sure,' Young said. 'They got enough water, they can make it across. Less chance o' runnin' into any more 'paches, too. That's what I'd try, I was runnin'.'

'Good,' gloated Burke Blantine. 'Then we got 'em.'

He turned in the saddle and gestured Pete Gilman forward.

'Pete,' he said. 'You ride on back a ways, you'll hit that long draw runs up to Picacho Pass. Head on down east an' you'll — '

' — pick up the trail to Santa Elizabeta, I know,' Gilman grinned. 'You want me to light a shuck thataway, huh?'

'Right,' Blantine said. 'Pass the word on to Dave Hurwitch to send men up to cover the Nogales road. They've got to cross it if Jud here is right.'

'That's rough country up there, boy,' Crumm said. 'They could lose an army up there they tried to.'

'Tell Hurwitch the price is doubled,'

snarled Blantine. 'Two thousand for the man that kills them!'

'You better warn them boys to play it careful,' Crumm advised. 'Your Daddy's with them, remember.'

'Tell them!' Blantine ordered. 'Tell them we're goin' to flush those bastards out o' these mountains like quail, an' all they got to do is take them!'

Gilman nodded, 'I'll pass the word,' he said. Then he pulled the head of his horse around and thundered off back along the route they had already traversed.

Blantine turned to face Young.

'Let's ride,' he yelled.

Young pushed his horse forward into the lead, half-leaning from the saddle, his keen eyes picking up the deep-cut hoof marks made by the horses of the fugitives as they had headed up the long steep rise into the mountains. The others swung into a straggled posse behind the tracker.

'That Jud,' Crumm wheezed as they moved on up into the mountains. 'He could track a trout in a river.'

'He better be as good as you say, Olan,' Blantine rasped. 'We lose them, an' you're goin' to be shy one tracker.'

Up in front, Young spat a long stream of tobacco juice at a surprised jackrabbit. If he had heard what Burke Blantine said, he gave no sign of it.

★ ★ ★

Up ahead, Vaughan and Gates crested a high rise, Yancey Blantine in tow behind them. Angel hauled his horse to a stop on the crest and let them go on a hundred yards or so. He turned back, his keen eyes searching the broken land behind them. A solid jumble of rock and boulder, interspersed here and there with flatter stretches floored with gritty sand and gravel stretched away as far as the eye could see. Up here, the sun was stronger, but the slight breeze cooled the body and skin. It was only when you stopped moving you felt the tingling burn of the sun.

The land dropped slowly away down to the lower levels from which they had climbed, scarred and twisted, gullied and uneven, spotted by stands of sparse timber and here and there on the higher mountain slopes a long grey fall of stone lay like a petrified river where winter avalanches had ripped the topsoil away from the shoulders of the hills.

A quick glance showed him that the others were now perhaps half a mile ahead, still moving upwards, still pointing towards the north. He remained motionless, letting his eyes take in the whole panorama before him rather than trying to focus on any one area; he knew this was the best way to spot anything alien moving in the vast wilderness. The peripheral vision picked out a rider or an animal far more quickly than the most assiduous concentration, and so he let his eyes swing forward and then back, across the empty land.

He saw them coming about ten minutes later.

They were like a vague blob, changing shape sinuously, the details shimmered and dispersed by the sunlight, so that from this huge distance they looked like a small swarm of bees skimming the surface of some vast rock-strewn pool. The pursuers disappeared then, riding down into a fold in the ground, a faint trace of dust marking their passage. Minutes later he saw them again, coming up to the crest of the deep arroyo they had traversed, nearer now, so that he could see individual riders, could roughly count their numbers.

'Twelve at least,' he muttered. His hand touched the saddle-bags behind the cantle of his saddle absently.

Another look over his shoulder showed him that the other three were now hauled in, waiting for him on the crest of another rise about three quarters of a mile ahead. He nodded. It was good to ride with men who didn't need to be told what to do. Until he turned and came after them, Gates and Vaughan would wait on where they were. A long way back the pursuing riders dipped down yet again into another arroyo, and still Angel waited. His mouth was drawn into a thin line and there was a decisive hardness around his eyes. He waited until they came up out of the arroyo, much nearer now, near enough for him to be able to pick out details: the colour of the horses, the red checkered shirt on one of the riders. Now Angel moved. He rode the horse back and forward along the rim of the crest, forward again and back until he knew that the riders coming after them could see him clearly. From afar he heard them yelling, and then saw a puff of smoke, followed by the flat bang of a sixgun.

There was no earthly possibility that anyone in the vengeful gang coming after them could have hit him from such a distance, so Angel knew that the shot was merely a gesture, a sign that he had been seen as he had intended to be seen. Once more he let the horse walk along the rim, and then he neck-reined it around, putting the animal to a run, clattering across the slatey ground towards where Gates and Vaughan waited.

When he came up to them, they turned their horses to move on, but Angel shook his head.

'They're getting some close, Frank,' Gates observed. There was no complaint or criticism in his voice. He was just stating a fact.

'I know it,' Angel said. 'Chris, you want to scout on up ahead and see if you can get a fix on two peaks, one o' them shaped like a man with a baby on his shoulders?'

'That's Apache Point,' Blantine put in. 'Head of Apache Canyon.'

'I know it,' Angel said brusquely. 'Get going, Chris.'

Vaughan nodded and wheeled his pony around, setting off at a flat run. Gates raised his eyebrows at Angel. 'Let the dog see the rabbit,' Angel said.

'Long as he don't snaffle him,' Gates replied, 'it's fine with me.'

'You're a fool, Angel!' snapped Yancey Blantine. 'You can't outrun my boys, especially if — ' His jaws snapped shut, and a cunning sneer touched his face.

'Especially if we head into Apache Canyon, you were going to say?' Angel supplied. 'That it?'

'You got your own lessons to learn, Angel!' snarled the old man. 'I aim to have the last laugh when my boys catch up on you.'

'Maybe you'll give me some of what you gave Dick Gould in Stockwood?' Angel said. 'That what you've got in mind?'

'Be a pleasure, Angel,' the old man said, an evil grin on his face. The bristly eyebrows concealed his eyes, but Angel knew that the light of devilish anticipation would be in them, the certain sureness that when he, Blantine, got the men who had so easily outwitted and humiliated him in his power, he would show them less mercy than he would show a coyote caught pulling down a yearling.

'Don't hang by your toes waiting,' Angel said humourlessly.

Up ahead of them they saw Chris Vaughan pull his pony back on its heels and wave his arm vigorously. They kicked the horses into a gallop and when they got up there along-side him, they could see the peculiarly shaped rock to which Angel had referred.

It hung poised on the edge of the mountain, misshapen and ugly, the red stone eroded by the winds of centuries until it had been shaped into a squat, menacing figure not unlike a seated Buddha, and which, when the sun hit it at a certain angle as now, bore a startling resemblance to the figure of a crouched man, rotund and jovial, with what might have been a child of three or four sitting on his shoulders. Apache Point! Angel blessed the hours he had spent poring over every map of the area that the Topographical Department and the Army had been able to let him study. Beyond the monstrous deformation of rock lay a gorge, long and narrow, deep and dark, which led upwards and slightly to the east, up into the final crest of the Santa Eulalias, opening at its far end into a wide and sandy declivity that led down towards the malpais, the open desert to the west of Santa Elizabeta.

'Take the old man on in,' Angel told Vaughan. 'An' don't turn your back on the old bastard for a second. If he gives you any hassle, shoot his eyes out.'

Vaughan grinned. 'Be a pure pleasure,' he said. 'You hear me, Blantine?'

'I hear you, sonny,' Blantine said. 'I aim to remember everything you ever said to me. When my boys catch us up, you'll pay mighty dear for every word. Mighty dear.'

'Talk, talk, talk, again,' Vaughan said shaking his head. 'Come on, Granpa!' He whacked Blantine's horse across the rump with the flat of his hand, grinning as the animal scooted across the rocky stretch of ground towards the darkened entrance of the canyon.

'We'll be along!' Angel shouted, and Vaughan waved a hand to show that he had heard. Then Angel swung down from his saddle, and unfastened the saddlebags, lifting from them two, four, six, seven canisters. He looked at Gates and Gates looked at him.

'Naughty boy,' Gates said, grinning. 'If you're thinkin' what I think you're thinkin'.'

'Take the far side,' Angel told him.

14

The sight of their quarry had galvanised the pursuers.

Without thought to the condition of the horses, Burke Blantine led his men at a punishing pace up the steadily rising slope after Angel and his companions. Young had fallen back now to join the main body of the riders: there was no need for tracking the fleeing men since there was only one direction in which they could now be heading.

'Apache Canyon!' Blantine had shouted. 'They're headin' for Apache Canyon!'

He said it like a man who finally knew his enemies have been delivered into his hands, and now he spurred his lathered horse mercilessly, flogging the animal into a faltering run, forcing the rest of them to keep up with his punishing pace.

Half an hour's riding brought them to the rim on which Angel had walked his horse, and here Olan Crumm called the cavalcade to a milling halt.

'Goddammit, Olan, why you stoppin' now?' screeched Blantine. 'They're no more'n two, three miles ahead of us!'

'Lissen, boy,' Crumm said, sweating profusely, his voice thin from the pounding ride. 'You aimin' to go after 'em on foot, yo're goin' the right way about it. These hosses is damn' near done for.'

'Won't hurt none to walk 'em a spell, Burke,' put in Ahern. 'Us neither.'

Blantine looked at them all, his lips curling with contempt.

'What is this?' he scoffed, 'some kind of animal-lovers' convention? You think I give a damn about the horses? That's my father those bastards have got with them, in case you've all forgot what you come up here for. You think I give a damn whether — '

'All I'm sayin' is we got to just give the hosses a breather, boy,' Crumm said, gently, breaking in on Blantine's wild speech. 'Now don't let's you an' me argue 'bout a li'l ol' thing like that.'

Blantine looked at the fat man and saw the steel beneath the layers of blubber, the killer under that seemingly bland exterior, and a cool breeze seemed to touch his body. He had overstepped the mark and Olan Crumm was letting him down easy. Without Crumm he could not continue the pursuit successfully. All right, he thought to himself. All right. There can be a reckoning when we get the Old Man back. Then we'll see who gives the orders, fat man. But he said:

'Olan, you're right, an' I'm a fool. Only let's keep movin'.'

'Why, sure, boy,' Crumm said. There was only the faintest gleam of triumph in his eyes but Burke Blantine saw it and marked it down as an additional penalty for Crumm to pay when the reckoning was presented. Fuming inwardly, cursing his own impotence — why hadn't he called the fat man out, shot him down like the tub of lard he was? — Burke Blantine settled back in the saddle, letting his horse pick its way up the shelving slope and on around the shoulder of the mountain, seething, plotting, taking his revenge a thousand times and then a thousand times again on the fat man in his own imagination.

'Apache Canyon, sure enough,' Jud Young announced.

Up ahead, they could see the jutting pile of deformed rock, the curiously leering expression on the stone 'face', the humped figure of the child on the back of the man etched sharp by the afternoon sun.

'They sure are makin' it easy for us,' Crumm said. There was a trace of suspicion in his voice, a slight unease that Blantinc quickly caught.

'It worry you goin' into the canyon, Olan?' he jeered. 'You reckon they aim to bushwack us? Climb up the cliffs, mebbe, an' shoot down at us?' He let a sneering laugh escape his lips.

'You don't got to tell me they ain't

nowhere in the canyon for them to hole up on us, boy,' Crumm said. 'I ain't worried none 'bout that.'

'What's botherin' you, boss?' Young asked. As usual he totally ignored Burke Blantine, who might not have been there or even spoken as far as Young's recognition of his leadership was concerned. Young worked for Olan Crumm; he wasn't about to take any shit from a layabout kid who wouldn't know how to follow a train to a station if you put him on the railroad lines.

'Don't rightly know, Jud,' Crumm said. 'It's all jest a mite over-easy for my taste.'

Young nodded. 'You want I should go take a look?'

'Might be a wise thing,' Crumm said. 'I'm takin' it you ain't got no objections, Burke?'

'Not me,' grinned Blantine. 'You go right on ahead, Olan. Take all day. Take all week if you like. My Daddy ain't goin' to fret none that you're spendin' all this time pussyfootin' around, now is he?' He let his grin widen into a sarcastic sneer. 'He's a-goin' to say: that Olan Crumm, he's a right keerful man, an' that's the kind I admire. Never takes a chance. Fifteen men chasin' three, but Olan, he jest nacherly wants to check everythin' twice afore he makes a move.'

'All right, all right,' Crumm snapped, his florid face flushed now with anger at Blantine's jibes. 'Let it be, Jud. We'll go on in after 'em.'

They kicked the horses into movement, and headed forward into the open ground lying before the entrance to Apache Canyon. It was cooler here; the rock formations leaped upwards in twisted, scoured cliffs, angled sharply, shading the ground. Inside the canyon it was blue dark and there was a chill dankness in the air, the slow seepage of water touching the face of one of the cliffs. Now on both sides of the riders the beetling walls rose starkly towards the burning heavens. The sound of their horses' hoofs echoed back at them from the stark granite.

Further along, the defile opened up slightly, and they entered a wider, open space where the seepage from the cliffs had formed a brackish pool of water. There were fresh tracks in the soft earth and Young eyed them expertly.

'All four o' them,' he said. He pointed on up the canyon and Blantine nodded, begrudging even the time it took for his horse to drink. He yanked the animal's head up away from the slimy pool and led the way up the canyon, the others pulling their horses into line after him, heading for the narrowest point of the defile now, their eyes warier, the very stillness of the place touching the edges of their nerves. Some of the riders fingered their sixguns nervously. Even with the assurance that no one could ambush them from these smooth and plantless cliffs, they still looked at each other and then up towards the top of the canyon where the brazen sky watched impassively.

Gene Johnson was riding drag, and it was he who screamed.

Every man in the gang stiffened in the saddle for Johnson's scream was that of a man in mortal fear, and he was looking upwards and from where he was looking, from the place their terrified eyes swivelled to see, they watched the entire wall of the canyon split away from the cliff with a terrible cracking boom, and they saw the whole thing lean over in a slow, awful, booming, rapidly crackling, thunderously tumbling, clattering, terrorizing, astonishing arc and then there was panic.

Eight men never even got their horses moving. They disappeared under a thousand tons of boulders, crashing giant slabs of granite that smashed to earth with impacts that made the ground shake. Johnson, the one who had screamed, was on the far side of the fall. His horse simply leaned right over backwards in its terror, unreasoning in its attempt to get away from the awful destruction, and it rolled as it hit the ground, and Johnson was underneath it. The high pommel, leather-covered and strengthened with steel, ground right through the centre of his chest and the terrified horse crushed the life out of its rider as if he had been a fly. Of the seven men in the van, only Burke Blantine escaped injury completely. Dave Ahern was swept out of his saddle by a piece of rock the size of a flat car and smashed against the canyon wall in a tattered mess of ruined tissue and bone. A boulder that whined angrily, humming viciously horizontal at a height of four feet from the ground neatly tore through Jud Young's thigh, throwing him screaming in agony from the saddle, writhing on the ground in the incredible noise and turmoil. Dust rose fifty feet in the air and the clattering rumble of rock moving down the new cliff face went on as stones whickered through the air and huge rocks bounced around the canyon floor like rubber balls. One of Crumm's men rose coughing from the dirt, his right arm dangling like a broken stick. He reeled towards the fallen body of the man who had been riding next to him, and who was cursing weakly and pushing ineffectually at a boulder which had rolled on to his foot. The scream of a terrified horse pierced the subsiding din and Burke Blantine lurched through the haze, eyes wild and mad in the dust-coated face, shouting hoarsely the names of his companions.

'Jesus, Jesus, Jesus, Jesus,' Young was yelling. There was a widening pool of blood around his thigh where he lay on the ground and Burke Blantine stood there aghast at the terrible sight of the man. He watched helplessly as Young tried to stanch the pulsing bright red flow, his hands spattered with his own blood, and could not move.

After a few moments Young slid sideways into the pool of his own blood and lay there retching. Then his eyes widened and the man screamed, fingers scrabbling at the dirt. Young managed to get to his feet. The superhuman effort terrified Burke Blantine, and Young saw him and the half-dead eyes asked him for help he could not give. Young stood there in the dust choked canyon, a monstrous vision on one leg, his whole lower body bathed in blood and dirt. Then, he fell again and before he hit the ground he was dead.

Now the dust began to settle in the canyon and Burke Blantine saw Olan Crumm on the ground, lying curiously twisted beside the still twitching body of his crushed horse. Blantine ran across to the fat man, whose eyes were wide open, staring at the sky above.

'Dynamite,' Crumm said. There was no expression in his voice. He said the word like a man who had known all along what would happen. 'God damn you, Burke!'

'I — I never — ' Blantine faltered.

'Dynamite!' Crumm repeated. Tears came into his eyes and to Blantine's astonishment the fat man began to laugh. The laugh went up a register and then another and became a maniacal shriek, the sound of a man who has looked into the very pit of hell. Then it died away and the fat man began to cry. Blantine helped him to his feet, grunting under the weight of the staggering, weeping man. They stood there in the utter desolation of jumbled rock and shattered stone, surrounded by the carnage wrought upon them. After a few minutes the two surviving riders stumbled over to join them.

Somewhere a bird tentatively tried to sing, then stopped.

And in the canyon there was only silence.

15

'You've killed my boys!' screamed Yancey Blantine. 'you've killed them all!'

'God willing,' Angel replied callously. 'They sure as hell needed killing.'

'God rot your festering soul, Angel!' the old man raved. 'I'll see you die slow for this. I'll strip the skin from your bones with my bare hands! I'll — '

Chris Vaughan unceremoniously stuck a dirty bandanna into the gaping mouth, cutting off Blantine's tirade in mid-sentence. Without ado, he tied a piggin' string around Blantine's head to keep the gag in place, and then dusted his hands in satisfaction.

'That ought to keep him quiet awhile,' he told the others. 'Damned if I know why I didn't do it ages ago.'

'You think all of them are dead, Frank?'

'Hard to tell,' Angel replied to Gates' question. 'I couldn't see down there too clearly once we set the charges off. Let's put it this way: we cut them down a few.'

'I couldn't see anyone moving down there,' Gates said. There was still a trace of awe in his voice. Standing with Angel on the rim of the canyon, watching that terrifying avalanche of granite breaking loose from the sides of the mountain, the way it had moved so slowly, so gracefully, then had shattered into a thousand, a thousand thousand terrible killing weapons, he had visualised himself beneath it, thought the thoughts of the men who had been below. They were killers, every one; renegades who rode beneath the colours of the Blantines, and who had killed innocent men and women on the old man's orders. Even so . . . a shudder touched Gates' huge frame. There were ways a man would choose to die, and that awful death in Apache Canyon was not one he would want to have had to face.

'It had to be done,' Angel told him, as if understanding what was going on in his companion's mind. They had clambered down the face of the cliff on two lariats which they had taken with them when they climbed up to set the charges. Vaughan had been waiting for them at the bottom, his face set and pale. It was then that the old man had burst into his tirade of threats and been so abruptly quietened.

'What now?' Vaughan asked.

'You go on ahead,' Angel told him. 'I'm going back to take a looksee.'

'Oh, no,' Vaughan said. 'You're having all the action. I didn't sign on to be a nursemaid to this cantankerous old goat.'

'You'll get all the action you can use before we get out of this country,' Angel promised him. 'Ride on to the end of the canyon and wait there. You too, Pearly. Don't argue, either of you. I can handle this alone.'

'We hear shooting, what do we do?' Gates asked.

'Get the hell out of here,' Angel told him harshly. 'I'm going to look, not to fight. Any sign of life back there and I'll be hightailing after you. Now, git!'

Vaughan looked at Gates and Gates looked at Vaughan and they sort of nodded to each other as Angel swung into the saddle.

'Get moving,' he told them.

'Sure, Frank,' Gates said. 'Soon as I get this rope coiled, here.'

Angel nodded and put the horse's nose towards the south. In a few moments he was around a bend in the canyon and they were out of sight. Some minutes later he saw the first signs of fallen rocks, smelled the fresh dust in the air. Tethering the horse, he moved forward on foot, edging now against the canyon wall, keeping to the shadowed foot where the blue darkness was deeper, testing each foothold before he put his weight on it. There were huge boulders all over the place and he could see nothing moving. Crouched low, moving as silently as an

Apache, he gained the shelter of one boulder, then eased around it. Another stood to his right and he slithered across to it. Beyond it a jumble of rock rose twenty, thirty feet above him, shattered and creviced from the explosion and the fall. He moved around this sheltering boulder and then upwards, always keeping the southern side of the rocks furthest from him, gaining height by which he could see down the canyon where the devastation had been the worst. Suddenly he froze; he heard voices.

'Easy, boy,' he heard someone say.

'I'm doin' the best I can,' someone else said, a whine in his voice.

'That leg don't look too good, Mr Crumm,' a third voice added.

'Dammit, I know that, Bert!' snapped the first voice.

Angel eased a little further around the sheltering rock. He was about eight or nine feet above them and to the right of where they were, he reckoned, although it was difficult to be sure. The resonances of the canyon wall made fixing positions extremely difficult. He edged a fraction further forward and then he could see them.

A huge, fat man sat with his back against a boulder, his clothing tattered and his jowly face streaked with sweat and dirt. At his feet knelt a younger man, whose face vaguely reminded Angel of someone. Of course! One of the Blantine boys, Burke most likely. But where were the others? There were only four men down there on the canyon floor. He tried to see further down the canyon, but hesitated; if he leaned out further and anyone looked this way, he would be easy to see. The fat man gave a curse.

'Easy, there, Burke!' he hissed. 'That hurts like hell!'

'Looks like you bruk your ankle, Mr Crumm,' the man called Bert said.

'Sure is swelled up bad,' Blantine said. 'I'll try an' bind it up the best I can, Olan.'

'Here, use this,' the fourth man said.

He was a rangy man of about thirty, and he limped forward, favouring his right leg. 'Funny you got your ankle busted up like that, Mr Crumm, an' me with that danged great rock fallin' on me on'y got kinda scraped . . . '

'Damn funny!' Crumm snarled. 'See me laughin', Henry, see me laughin'!'

'Sorry, Mr Crumm,' the man said. 'No offence.'

Angel leaned back against the sheltering rock. Was this all of them? Had the avalanche wiped out eleven men? He edged forward again as Blantine spoke.

'We got to go on after them,' he said. 'More so now than ever.'

'Leave 'em to Hurwitch, Burke,' the fat man said. 'We're sure in no shape to chase them, even if we had hosses.'

'There's two hosses OK, Mr Crumm,' the man called Henry offered. 'Me an' Bert could hold on up here until you was able to send someone up after us, I reckon.'

'Sure thing,' said Bert.

Angel frowned in his hideout. Where were the horses? Perhaps he could pick them off. That would effectively stop any sort of pursuit behind them. Who was Hurwitch? What had the fat man meant when he said Blantine could leave Hurwitch to take care of things? The lines of concentration deepened between Angel's brows and he moved his foot for better purchase on the thin ledge upon which he was standing. As he did so he felt the stone break, a piece of soft slate turning beneath his foot and destroying his balance. The slate clattered down the side of the bare rock and Angel jumped, out into the open, the four men on the canyon floor already moving for their guns.

Angel's leap took him seven or eight feet, a clawing, off-balance try for the shelter of a boulder up against the wall of the canyon. He hit the ground on his hands and knees rolling headfirst into a somersault, and the first bullet smacked into the rock above him as Burke Blantine got into action.

Olan Crumm scuttled with incredible speed for the rocks behind him as Burke Blantine, crouching in the centre of the canyon floor, fired again at Angel, cursing as his bullet once more smashed rock splinters out of the boulder around which Angel was squirming.

The two other men, Bert and Henry, reacted instinctively. Pulling their hand-guns they ran straight at Angel, firing as they came. He saw them coming and stopped rolling, moving right and then left in a feinting crouch, then came up off the ground with the gun in his hand, his left hand moving back across the hammer once, twice. Bert and Henry were no more than five feet away from Angel when he fired and his fanned shots blasted them off their feet as if they were rag dolls. Henry screamed as he ploughed sideways into the gravel, the wicked stones tearing at his already lifeless face. The man Bert went backwards as if he had been kicked over, his bootsoles flashing briefly white, dust-coated and scuffed, and his body hit the ground with an impact that scattered dust. Angel was moving sideways even before Henry's body stopped falling, and he threw a hasty shot at Burke Blantine, who was now dashing for the shelter of a boulder. The shot whined off into infinity, its thin ricocheting scream loud in the gloom. Angel got the thickness of a huge boulder between himself and Blantine, and then felt the whole world fall on his head. Olan Crumm, neatly hidden behind a big rock on Angel's right, opened up, and his first shot smacked Angel's skull lightly in passing, so close that Death looked around and then passed on. But the stunning force of even a creasing shot will knock a steer to its knees, and Angel spun round, the gun flying from his hand. Senses reeling, blood trickling inside his collar, Angel fought to regain control of his body but all he could do was to struggle to his knees. His sight was blurred and he could not see his gun. He did not realize that he was out in the open, scrabbling blindly in the gravelled dust. He did not know that Burke Blantine was coming out from behind the rock, the sixgun in his hand levelled. Angel had momentarily lost track of time and space, and in the moment that his head cleared, in the moment that the blurring mist went from his eyes, he knew he was lost. He looked up and saw Burke standing over him. There was madness and a killing lust in the exulting eyes.

'Olan!' Blantine yelled. 'Come out here an' watch me kill this sonofabitch.'

Angel saw his own gun. It was lying in the dirt about four feet away. Too far: he had no hope of reaching it. But he knew he was going to try.

'Burke,' Crumm yelled.

'Now,' Blantine hissed. 'Now!' Angel heard the triple click as the gun was cocked.

'Hey!' called Chris Vaughan from ten feet away.

Burke Blantine whirled instinctively towards the sound of Vaughan's voice and Vaughan shot him in the heart. Blantine's gun went off as he was smashed off his feet by the force of the bullet and Angel yelled, 'Chris, get down!' as Crumm fired from behind the rocks. Angel saw dust puff off Vaughan's shirt and Chris sat down weakly on the rocks as Angel rolled in one continuous co-ordinated movement that brought him over his gun and up with the gun in his hand firing and his two bullets blasting the triumphant grin off the face of Olan Crumm, splattering the thing that had been the fat man back against the boulders, headless and obscene.

Angel stood upright, letting the adrenalin dissolve, taking one deep breath before turning around and running across to where Chris sat on the rocks, his hand on his body at the front, just below the ribcage.

He was smiling foolishly, in shock from the wound.

'Never learn, Frank,' he said, lightly. 'I never learn.'

He fell soundlessly into Angel's arms and Angel ripped the shirt open. The wound was raw and ragged, and when Angel put his hand around in back of his friend, it came away slippery with blood.

'You — idjut,' he said softly to the unconscious man.

Then Gates came scrambling over the rocks and took the whole scene in with one comprehending glance. His eyes fell on Chris Vaughan lying pale and bloody in the deepening gloom of the canyon. He bent down and picked up the wounded man as gently and tenderly as if Chris had been a baby and looked at Angel.

'Is he gonna die?' he said.

'I don't know,' Angel replied.

'Oh, Jesus,' Gates said.

16

'They're waiting for us,' Gates announced.

The first full strength of the sun was yellowing the sky where they could see it up beyond the towering walls of the canyon. They had remained in its safety all night, doing the best they could with Vaughan's wound, binding it tightly with strips torn from their shirts and undershirts, making Chris as comfortable as possible. He had gotten fevers, tossing and moaning in his sleep, sweat starting from him like running water. Sometimes he had moaned, a long low cry of pain. Gates had sat with him all night, not sleeping. At dawn, he had nodded to Angel, and slid away into the twilight, prowling along the edges of the canyon towards the place where the rocky walls fell away, and the canyon opened out on to the falling shale slope that ran east towards Santa Elizabeta and north into the malpais. He could see the lights of the town twinkling faintly in the clear desert air. For all his size, Gates could move like an Indian when he had to, and he watched immobile in the rocks until he saw movement, heard the rusty cough of a man who had lain in the open all night. He saw that man, then spotted another and another. He projected a line in his head and swung his eyes along it, grunting each time he spotted something alien that meant the presence of a man, one behind a boulder, another prone in a gully, a third hidden under a yucca. There were men bayed all around the exit of the canyon, waiting for them to come out. There was no other exit. Behind them, the canyon was blocked. In front, a murderous ambush awaited. He eased his way out of there and back along the shadowed walls of the canyon.

'How many?' Angel said.

'Hard to tell,' Gates reported. 'Ten, a dozen, maybe.'

Angel nodded.

With Vaughan wounded there was no way they could make a run for it, or even make a fight of it. They were boxed in. Trying to get through the waiting line of men could only mean death for all of them. He looked at Yancey Blantine. The old man looked shrunken, very old. The bushy eyebrows were lowered over the lambent eyes, and the burly shoulders slumped. The death of his sons had taken all the fire out of the old man. Burke, the dashing, handsome Burke, had been his favourite. He did not know who else was dead: none of them did. But Angel had told him about the death of Burke and Olan Crumm.

He stood up, his decision made.

'Pearly, rig up a ten-minute fuse on the rest of those cans of blasting powder,' he said. 'Then tie them to Blantine's horse.'

Gates looked a question, but set about doing what Angel had told him. There were three cans. He rigged a looped truss for them, and dallied it around the cantle of the saddle behind where the old man would sit. From the saddle-bags he took a length of fuse, measured it roughly, frowning as he worked out the measurement, and fixed it inside one of the closely bound tins. Then he let it drop and turned towards Angel.

'No smoking,' he said.

While he had been busy with his task, Angel had been examining Chris Vaughan. In the growing light, Vaughan's face looked pinched and very pale. He was terribly weak, but he opened his eyes and grinned.

'Well,' he said. 'So I'm still here?'

'How you feeling, Chris?' Gates asked.

'Very fragile,' Vaughan replied. 'An' extremely stupid.'

'We got them all,' Angel told him. Vaughan nodded.

'Naturally,' he said.

'Chris, I never said thank you,' Angel said. 'If that's the right words. They sure don't seem like enough.'

'You could give me a kiss,' Vaughan grinned, then cursed as a stab of pain twisted his body. 'Damn an' blast!' He touched the pad of bandage on his side tentatively. 'Can I ride?'

'You shouldn't,' Angel replied. 'But you've got to. We're moving out.'

'There's more o' them waitin' for us,' Gates added.

'We — sure do — have jolly times together,' Vaughan said, sitting up and trying to get to his feet. His face was wet with sweat and he reeled and would have fallen had Gates not grabbed him. Vaughan leaned heavily on his companion.

'Whew!' he said. 'My belly feels like it's full of boiling oil.'

'Bullet went right through,' Angel said. 'But it tore you up some.'

'Damned well feels like it,' Vaughan gritted through his teeth. 'All right. Let go of me, you big slab o' beef.'

Gates stepped away, and Vaughan reeled again, but kept his feet. He looked at Angel and nodded.

'I can manage,' he said. His jaw muscles were knotted and the sweat had drenched his shirt, dark stains of moisture plastering the garment to him.

'How do we play it, Frank?' Gates asked.

'You ride double with Chris,' Angel said. 'Lead his horse. We'll have to let the packmule go.'

'And then?'

'Stay as close to me as you can!' Angel ordered. 'It's going to be touch and go anyway.'

He turned to Yancey Blantine, and yanked the old man to his feet. Blantine snarled his annoyance, but Angel ignored the hatred in the old man's eyes.

'Listen to me!' he snapped. 'Because your life depends on it!'

'Go to hell!' Blantine snarled.

Angel slapped Yancey Blantine across the face. He hit the man contemptuously once, and then again with the back of his hand.

'Listen!' he snapped. Blantine relapsed into sullen silence.

'You see those canisters on your saddle?' Angel demanded.

Blantine nodded. 'I see them.'

'There's enough blasting powder in them to blow you to Kingdom Come,' Angel informed him. 'And a ten-minute fuse: you see it?'

Again Blantine nodded.

'We're going to ride out there now to where your friends are waiting,' Angel said. 'And you're going to call them off.'

'Sure,' sneered Blantine. 'Like Hell!'

'You'll do it,' Angel assured him. 'Because you'll only have those ten minutes. Ten minutes, Blantine! You hear me? I'm going to light that fuse and ride out there with you. We all are. You call off your dogs or I ground hitch you on the pony and let the fuse burn. You'll sit there and watch it burn right up to the powder, and then you'll be spread all over these mountains. So you better do some convincing talking!'

The old man looked at the blasting powder canisters strapped to his saddle and then back at Angel.

'Yo're bluffin'!' he snapped. 'You want me alive, you said so yourself!'

'I want me alive more,' Angel said. 'Get up!'

'I ain't — ' Blantine began, but again Angel slapped him, again his contemptuous hand rocking the man's head from side to side. Blood trickled from Yancey Blantine's broken lips. He spat.

'Get up!' Angel told him, and with a curse, the old renegade swung awkwardly up into the saddle. With a few deft loops, Angel bound his hands to the pommel of the saddle. Then he tied the reins of Blantine's horse to the pommel of his own saddle.

'Better rehearse what you're going to say, Blantine,' he said. 'You haven't got long.'

Blantine said nothing. He watched with murderous eyes as Angel and Gates helped the wounded Vaughan into his saddle. Vaughan sat on his horse like a sack of flour.

'Let's move,' Angel said, and they kneed the horses into motion, moving on down the canyon and towards the widening exit where the morning sunlight painted the forbidding; walls a brightening shade of reddish gold.

As they approached the open declivity at the end of the canyon, he heard someone give a hoarse shout, and turned to Blantine.

'Start shouting, Blantine,' he said coldly, and put a match to the fuse. It spluttered for a moment and then started to hiss as the flame caught. Angel held the fuse in his hand and kneed the horse forward into the open. Gates came up close behind him, holding the reins of Vaughan's horse.

'Boys!' screeched Yancey Blantine. 'Don't shoot, boys! Hold your fire!'

They moved slowly forward, and as they did they saw men rising from their hiding places, guns ported and ready, the sunlight catching bright flashes of metal in a long semi-circle in front of the four riders coming out of the canyon.

'Pa!' someone yelled. 'Pa!'

They saw a huge giant of a man stumbling towards them up the hill, sixgun in his hand. Behind him came a portly, black clad man with the dead-white face of the professional gambler.

'Tell them to keep away!' snapped Angel. 'Talk, damn you!'

'Gregg!' screamed Yancey Blantine. 'Gregg, keep back. They got a fuse burning here! I'm sittin' on a bomb! Get back, get back!'

'Listen to me, down there!' Angel yelled. His words bounced back off the canyon walls in the silence. The Blantine men ringed around them stood ready, guns cocked, waiting.

'There's a ten minute fuse burning in my hand!' Angel yelled. 'And about four minutes of it have gone! We're heading down the hill past you, and we're coming fast! Anyone tries to stop us, I'll whip Blantine's horse up and let go of the fuse. You want to see him blown to pieces in front of you?'

He kept the horses moving inexorably forward, heading for the shelving slope that led downwards and away from Santa Elizabeta. Off to the north he could see the flat shimmer of the desert.

'Is he bluffin', Yancey?' shouted the white faced man.

'Goddammit, Hurwitch, get your men out o' here!' screamed Yancey Blantine. Angel was counting out loud, loud enough to be heard only by Blantine, and he had said six. The old man could hear the hiss of the fuse, and he was afraid to look and see how short it was.

'We're movin',' Angel shouted. 'Anyone tries anything, and I let the old man go!'

'Pa!' the giant shouted. 'You all right, Pa?'

'Gregg, boy!' Yancey Blantine sobbed. 'For God's sake get back away an' let them through. Let them through!'

Angel looked over his shoulder at

Gates and nodded. Chris Vaughan set his lips, and pressed a hand to his wounded side.

'Yeeeeeeeeeeeeehah!' Angel yelled, and gave his horse a vicious cut across the withers with the double reins. The stinging slap made the horse jump to a running gallop, dragging Yancey Blantine's horse along. The old man snatched at the pommel with his bound hands, and all four riders rocketed down the shallow slope, dust climbing up behind them, the astonished ambushers watching helplessly as they headed on down the slope and then the tableau broke.

'Hold your fire!' yelled Hurwitch. 'Nobody fire at them! Don't take no chances on hitting the Old Man!'

The four riders were at the edge of the steep declivity now that slanted down to the flat sandy arroyo whose twisted course led off north towards the malpais.

The ambushers were not idle, either. They ran to their tethered horses, swinging into the saddle and milling into a tightly bunched mass, the horses curvetting and snorting as their riders held them back from the pursuit.

'What are we waiting for?' yelled one of the men.

'Shut your stupid face!' snapped Hurwitch. 'We give them their ten minutes, and ten minutes more if we got to. They can't outrun us!'

'None o' you is to take any chances with my Pa's life!' Gregg Blantine told them ponderously. 'You hear me?'

They looked at him and nodded, or gave a muttered assent. Although every one of them knew Gregg was a mite slow on the uptake, they had also seen him use those terrible hamlike fists on men. Gregg did not know what it was like to lose a fight. None of them had ever seen the man who could stand up to him, and none of them had any inclination to try to be the first.

'There they go!' one of Hurwitch's men shouted.

'Headin' straight for the malpais,'

Pete Gilman added. He gigged his horse up alongside Gregg Blantine's. 'We'll get 'em, Gregg,' he said.

Gregg Blantine nodded.

'I'll get them,' he said. It was not a correction and Gilman did not take it that way. He knew that what Gregg Blantine meant was that no matter what happened, no matter what the cost, nor how long the pursuit, Gregg Blantine had arrived at his own decision. Nothing short of death would now alter it. Gilman looked at the giant and shivered: he did not envy the man who fell into Gregg Blantine's hands at any time. The man who had hurt Gregg Blantine's father could scarcely hope to die in less than agony when the huge giant finally caught up with him.

'What you reckon happened to Burke an' the others?' Hurwitch asked him.

'Hard to tell,' Gilman said. 'Mebbe they lost them in the mountains. I figgered they'd go on in after them at Apache Canyon. Could be they decided to drive them out, or mebbe just sit at the other end to make sure they didn't double back.'

'Could be,' Hurwitch admitted. 'All the better for my boys.'

'How d'you mean?' Gilman asked.

'Well . . . ' Hurwitch grinned evilly, his face taking on the shape and deathly malice of a skull, 'one of us is goin' to pick up the $2,000 Burke promised to the man who brung in this Angel feller.'

Gilman grinned.

'You better shoot him good an' dead, Dave,' he said wickedly. 'You take him alive, an' you'll have to fight with Gregg for him.' He gestured towards the big man, who was leaning forward in his saddle, watching the dots which were the fleeing quartet with burning intensity.

'Thanks a lot,' Hurwitch grated, 'but no thanks!'

He neck-reined the horse around and went up to the front of the bunched riders.

'OK,' he said. 'Spread out when we get down to the arroyo. I want a

Comanche sickle half a mile across. Them bastards might just try to double back.'

His riders nodded, and fidgeted with the reins. They were eager to get started.

'Let's go!' yelled Hurwitch.

The phalanx of riders moved off down the shelving slope, sliding and sidling until they had descended to the level, sandy floor of the riverbed below. Then they moved away from each other. In a few moments they were spread into a formation somewhat like a letter C on its side, the Comanche sickle, the raiding formation of the warlike Indians which let nothing pass through it, which drove its prey before it like a scythe. Harness jingling, sunlight gleaming on the ported carbines across their saddlebows, the hunters headed up towards the malpais, the tracks of the fleeing men plain in the sandy ground. And at the centre of the arc of riders was Gregg Blantine, hunched forward still in the saddle, eyes burning like deepset coals in his expressionless face, fixed on the burning land ahead.

'My Gawd!' one of the riders exclaimed. 'Will you look at him?'

'Sure as hell wouldn't want that on my tail!' exclaimed his neighbour.

'Right,' said the first. 'He scares the shit outa me, an' he's on our side!'

They moved on into the sledging heat of the chiaroscuroed desert.

17

When they had covered about six miles, Vaughan fell off his horse. He did not cry out. One moment they were pushing at a steady canter through the open, burning land, concentrating upon simply covering ground, knowing their pursuers must already be moving up behind them. They hit a sharp slope down into a gully and crossing it, the horses jumped at the far side and Vaughan went backwards off his horse and lay in the sand, shaking his head.

In a moment Gates was out of the saddle and beside him, lifting Vaughan's head.

'No — good!' Vaughan managed.

'Come on.' Gates said. 'I'll carry you.' He put an arm under Vaughan's limp body and then cursed. When Angel swung down beside him he showed him the bloody hand.

'Get out of here,' Vaughan said weakly. 'Get — goin'!'

Gates shook his head stubbornly. 'I ain't leavin' him,' he said to Angel. His voice was truculent, as though he would fight about it.

'Yes. Yes — you are!' Vaughan managed. He made a gesture with his hand towards his body. 'All — busted open,' he managed. 'No. No — chance.' Angel just looked at him. Gates cursed.

'Get out of here,' Vaughan said. He made a supreme effort of will and sat up, the colour draining from his face as he did so. The smile he put on his face wrenched the guts of the two men watching him.

'That blasting powder,' he said. 'Give it to me. And — a — rifle.'

'No!' Gates shouted.

'Goddamn you, Pearly, do like I say!' Vaughan shouted. His outburst racked his body with pain, but he forced himself to get to his knees and then, agony on his face, every muscle screaming with the pain in his body, he stood up.

'Help me over to that rock,' he said. The muscles along his jawline were bunched like stones and his hair was soaking wet with perspiration.

'Help me, damn you!'

Gates helped him. Angel stripped the canisters of blasting powder from Blantine's saddle and unsheathed his own carbine, a .44.40 Winchester. He ran across the arroyo towards Gates, who was easing Vaughan to the ground in the shelter of a sloping rock that leaned against the far side of the gully they had been trying to cross.

'Give me that,' Vaughan said. He was going on sheer nerves now and they could see a pulse throbbing in his temple. He took the carbine and jacked a shell into the breech.

Then he pointed up to the rim of the gully.

'Get me up there! Behind the rock.'

'Goddammit, Chris — ' Gates burst out.

'Pearly, you argue any more and so help me I'll — ' Vaughan's iron control faltered, and a fit of coughing racked his frame. They saw blood fleck his lips. Vaughan wiped the bright red spots away with the back of his hand, and as gently as they could, they lifted him up behind the rock. Off across the empty desert nothing moved, but they all knew the pursuers were out there. Vaughan looked back across the gully at Yancey Blantine, sitting on the ground where Angel had unceremoniously thrown him as he ran back.

'That old bastard!' Vaughan said. 'I'd've — liked to see him — hang.'

They saw his eyes swim and he teetered for a moment then pulled himself around.

'I can. I — can hold out, Frank,' he managed. 'Give you — some runnin' time . . . ' Again the wrenching cough seized him and Gates half lifted a hand, then let it drop. There was agony in his eyes too, but of a different sort, Angel thought.

'The powder,' Vaughan said. 'Toss it out there where — I can see it.' Gates lobbed the three tins out on to the open sand. One to the right, one in the middle, one to the left. Vaughan squinted along the barrel of the carbine. He nodded.

'*Bueno*,' he said. 'I can see th — ' He drew a breath and then let it out. The pain was burning him up, and his hands were trembling. He laid the carbine down on the hot rock.

'Move out,' he said.

When he saw them hesitate he began to curse them. Every obscenity he had ever learned poured out of him until they moved, and slid down the rock away from him. Vaughan nodded.

'Chris,' Angel said, tentatively.

Vaughan shook his head. 'No,' he said. 'There's no one.'

'The buttermilk and honey girl?'

'That's a pretty thought,' Vaughan called. His voice was lighter now, and the harshness was gone from it. 'Go on, get the hell out of here! You're

— wasting time!'

Angel raised a hand. Vaughan smiled and at that distance, his smile was the heartbreaking, boyish smile that they remembered. Angel fixed it in his mind and then turned away. He jerked Yancey Blantine to his feet and pushed him towards the horse. Blantine clambered up into the hurricane deck and then looked back across the gully towards Vaughan. He opened his mouth to speak, a sneer already fixed on his face, and as he did so he saw Angel's eyes.

'Say it,' Angel said quietly, 'just say it!'

Yancey Blantine was a renegade. He had killed men with his own bare hands, in terrible rages and in the bitterest of cold blood. He had stood by and watched the carnage his riders had wrought in Stockwood without a tremor but what he saw now in Angel's eyes froze his very marrow. He did not think he had ever seen the cold lust to kill so naked in a man's eyes and he recoiled, his lips trembling.

'Go!' Angel said to Gates.

The big man cast one last despairing glance at Chris Vaughan and then swung his horse around, riding blindly ahead of Angel and the tethered Blantine, his eyes misted with a pain he could not isolate.

They thundered off into the desert, the dust of their going sifting high and falling. Vaughan could hear it settle to the ground, a tiny hissing sound that touched the edges of his heightened consciousness. The pain was now a total entity below his ribcage. It burned like all the fires of hell inside him, as tangible as the rock slab he lay upon. The heat of the noon sunlight was terrible, now, yet he hardly felt it. Strange ghostly films drifted across his vision and once he lapsed into unconsciousness, rapping his forehead against the rock then jerking back to instant alertness, sweat dripping from his face and spotting the sandstone in front of his eyes.

'Come on,' he muttered to himself,

to the desert, to the pursuing renegades he could not see. 'Come on!'

A flicker of movement caught his eye. A kangaroo rat poked its nose out of its hole about ten feet in front of him, then wriggled out on to the sand. It moved away from the hole in its curious, hitchkicking gait. Vaughan grinned.

'You better get out o' here, friend,' he whispered. 'Gonna get some noisy shortly.'

The kangaroo rat heard his voice and scuttled squeaking for the safe shelter of a prickly pear. As it did, Vaughan heard the jingle of steel touching steel, the sound of harness, perhaps, or a spur touching a cinch ring. He tightened his grip on the carbine as the first rider came into view about forty yards away.

He let them get within twenty yards before he fired.

His first shot catapulted Dave Hurwitch out of the saddle and he levered the Winchester as fast as he could after that, ignoring the deep bite of the pain inside him, swinging the carbine around, dropping men from the backs of their horses with each shot, the sweat dripping off him and now the slow red pulse of blood brightening the makeshift bandages around his middle.

He saw now that they had come forward in a long arc and although he had dropped four of them in the first blasting volley, they were already moving in on him, bent low over the necks of their horses, firing as they came. Slugs whined past him and once he felt the slightest tug on his shirt and looked down surprised to see that blood was coursing down his arm. He felt nothing. A feverish exaltation gripped him and he levered the carbine again and fired, knowing he could not miss, there was no way he could miss. Again he fired and again and each time he heard the meaty sound of the slug smacking into the body of a horse, saw a man spin flailing to the ground. One man rose and ran for the shelter of a tall ocatillo, throwing himself behind it and Vaughan shot him in midair, knowing the man was dead as he hit the ground, grinning triumphantly to himself at the way he was shooting. The first wave of the riders came level with the canister of blasting powder in the centre dead ahead of him and he aimed very casually and fired and the air filled with the booming flash of the explosion. Sand and stones boiled up in a huge cloud and he thought he saw something tattered like a shirt flop to the ground, and then he waited no longer. They were all there in front of him now and he fired at the other canister of powder and then the third, the explosions almost simultaneous, a boom! and then another boom! There was a thin scream in the roaring hail of dirt and sand, but he could see nothing except the sifting pall of dirt. His eyes were unfocusing and he levered the action of the Winchester, swinging the barrel around seeking anything that moved, a faint smile on his lips. He never even saw Gregg Blantine rise out of the swirling dust and level his six-gun. When the remaining men came running forward they found Blantine standing over Vaughan's body. Even in death he was still smiling.

18

Nothing crossed the land of the Apaches that the Apache did not see. Scouts had charted the course of the fugitives, watched the dust of the pursuers. They had told it back in the village high in the Huachucas: how the huge mountain had fallen with the noise of many thunders. There were women there with cut arms mourning the three dead warriors killed in the box canyon.

The Apaches watched the white men impassively, biding time. From unseen hiding places, grim-faced warriors had watched the fight between Vaughan and the pursuers, and they had told it around the fires, calling him the brave one with the yellow hair. There was no surprise among them that the white-eyes killed each other; they had long since stopped being surprised at anything the white men did. But like children, they were intrigued by the chase unfolding across their hunting land. They who fled seemed to have nothing that they who followed could want. Unless it was the yellow dust which drove all white men insane. Yes, they nodded. It could be that.

They watched as the white men plunged further into the burning sea of sand and rock, past the place that all Apaches knew, the place from which it was too far to water.

Now the white men could not turn back but must go forward, and it was time. For the white men had the long guns that fired many times, Huin-jez-da they called them. Such guns were great prizes; an Apache would trade many horses to get such a weapon. Now Yosen had sent them into the desert for the Apaches to take. Pursuers or pursued: to the Apache it was all the same.

And so they came down out of the Huachucas, out of the cool heights where the wickiups lay along the banks of the trickling stream and down the scarred arroyos that tumbled towards the wasteland below. There were ten of them, moving easily behind their leader whose name in Apache was Ke-a'hchay, he whom the Mexicans had dubbed Saguarito, a warrior of great experience who was much respected among Apaches for he had been one of the Chiricahuas chosen to ride his pony over the grave of the dead Cochise.

The Apaches came on foot to the desert. They could cover thirty miles easily in their tireless jog trot during one day, and be ready at the end of it to fight if they needed to fight. Saguarito chose to wait until the morning. They made belly fires in sandy pits and warmed themselves over them against the chill of the desert night, and drank a little *tiswin*. Saguarito's plan was a simple one, as were all Apache fighting plans. They would circle around behind the pursuers and kill them first. The brave one with the yellow hair had killed six of them, and wounded another, the scouts had said. The remaining men would have many guns, some of them two of the Huin-jez-das. With those guns, Saguarito and his men would have no trouble with the three others who were left.

'*Enju!*' his men grunted in the darkness.

★ ★ ★

Gilman saw them come up out of the ground like ghosts and yelled a warning that echoed in the thin light of the dawn. The Apaches had lain all night in an arroyo not two hundred yards from the camp of the pursuers, and as the faint light touched the horizon they moved forward like wraiths, their bodies coated with the grey dust of the desert so that they were almost invisible, easing on their bellies towards the campsite where the white men were stirring, stretching legs and arms stiffened by the cold night and the many miles of riding.

Gregg Blantine tumbled out of his blankets, leaping to his feet and levering the action of his Winchester. He saw a running Apache hurl himself at Chaffee, and the white man and the Indian going over in a tumble of arms and legs, raising dust high and then they were everywhere, their thin ullulating screams pitched high to terrify their quarry. Pete Gilman dropped to the ground, his legs kicking high in agony, gutted by the swift sweep of a razor-edged knife, and then the white men's guns blasted and two Apaches who were running towards them went over sideways and down. Gregg Blantine ran towards Fred Little, who stood in the centre of the open campsite, the Winchester ported across his thigh, levering the action and firing as fast as he could. Blantine threw a shot at a running Apache who came arcing to meet him and the Apache kept coming and then he was on Blantine, knife arm raised high. Blantine let him come, using the Indian's weight to roll him over on his back, and his powerful legs came up in a wicked double kick that smashed into the Apache's groin as Gregg threw him backwards over his head. He leapt to his feet and put a bullet into the contorted face and then whirled around. Hand-to-hand struggles were going on here and there. Two men lay already dead on the ground. Fred Little was down on one knee, cursing as he tried to lever the action of his carbine with a right arm streaming blood.

'Get back!' Blantine yelled. 'Get to cover!'

The Apaches had evaporated back into the arroyo, but they were still there. Arrows whipped past the running white men and then a carbine that one of the Apaches had picked up boomed and Gregg Blantine saw Mark Chaffee falter as he ran, the legs going wobbly, and the tall rider slid to the ground, lying on his back with his body arching upwards in pain. Chaffee was yelling something wordless and then they were all behind the rocks, panting, sweating in the cool morning sunlight, the bright fullness of the day upon their faces and the Apaches down there somewhere in front of them.

The silence was enormous.

Gregg Blantine broke it with a vivid curse. And the Apaches came at them again. They came across the broken ground where the dead men lay in curiously twisted heaps, swift, crouching, running shapes zigzagging with deadly purpose towards the circle of rocks behind which the four men lay hidden.

They used their sixguns now, firing as fast as they could ear back the spurred hammers, blasting away at the wraith-like shapes in the clouding smoke and dust. Then the Apaches melted back and Gregg Blantine let his tensed muscles ease, wetting his lips. One of Hurwitch's riders was dead beside him. An arrow stuck obscenely from his neck where the collarbones came together, and its sparse feathers quivered ever so slightly in the touch of breeze that came off the desert. Fred Little was holding his right arm up for Ronnie Busch to tie with a bandanna.

'Right through,' Little said, his teeth tight against the pain.

'Hold on now,' Busch said and pulled the knotted bandanna tight.

Little's face went as white as flour and his eyes rolled up. He let his body relax against the rock, sweat springing to his forehead.

'Christ a' mighty,' he gasped.

'It's done,' Busch told him.

'Goddammed Injuns!' Gregg muttered. His companions realized that to Gregg's slow mind, the Apaches were an irritation — something which had come between him and the decision he had come to back at Apache Canyon: to catch up with Angel and kill him, to rescue Yancey Blantine. Anything else was a nuisance. It simply did not occur to Gregg Blantine that the Apaches would kill them all. His mind was incapable of conceiving the thought.

'Gregg,' Busch said. 'We're in a tight spot.'

'Goddammed Injuns,' Gregg said again. 'Whyn't they come on out where I can see 'em?'

Busch shook his head. In action, Gregg Blantine was a superb animal, the huge muscles and the giant body doing what Nature had built them for. Of cunning, of subtlety, Gregg knew nothing and would never learn. He had no thought of out-thinking any enemy. Gregg knew only one direction and that was forward.

Busch was not brave. He was a hired hand, and he had already seen his comrades die. They had died bloodily in Vaughan's ambush and two more were out there on the flat ground now, dead from Apache knives. Busch did not want to die the same way.

'Gregg,' he whispered urgently. 'We can't stay here an' let them get around behind us. We got to make a run for it!'

'Let 'em come,' Gregg snarled. 'Let 'em come!'

'No!' Busch told him, angrily. 'They'll cut us to pieces! Even if they don't they can just sit out there an' wait till we're crazy with thirst an' finish us off when they're ready. We got to go out after them or make a run for it.'

'He's right, Gregg,' Jerry Kershoe said, and Fred Little nodded.

'You see how many of them there was, Jerry?' Busch asked.

'Eight, ten, mebbe.'

'We got three,' Busch muttered. 'Seven to four. Could be worse.'

'Not much,' Little said flatly. 'Them's fightin' Apaches, Ron.'

'An' they got the hosses,' Little added.

'What do we do?' Kershoe hissed. 'What do we do?'

The answer was not long in coming. Saguarito gave a hoarse yell down in the arroyo and the remaining Apaches came in a widespread running line up over the rim, flat out in a long killing run, a last determined charge to reach the white men behind the thin shelter of the burning rocks.

19

The sound of the shots brought Angel instantly awake. Gates and Yancey Blantine sat up simultaneously and they all looked at each other in the grey light.

'Apaches?' Gates said.

'Got to be,' Angel told him.

'Apaches?' Blantine repeated dully. He got to his feet, madness in his eyes, an agonised shout escaping his lips. 'They're killing my boys?'

'They sure as hell aren't servin' 'em tea,' Angel told him. 'Get on your horse!'

'No!' screamed Yancey Blantine. 'No!'

Gates hit him with the barrel of his sixgun and the older man folded at the knees and slumped to the ground. Gates picked up the fallen renegade as if he had been a child and manhandled him into the saddle.

'We better burn shucks,' he said.

Angel nodded. It was not a matter of cowardice or bravery now but of pure survival. They had been given breathing space by the attack on their pursuers and they had to use it.

'Move!' he shouted to Gates. 'Kill the horses if you have to!'

Gates nodded to show he had heard. Their horses were in poor shape anyway, but now they would have to ride them until the animals dropped from exhaustion. When the Apaches were done, they would come after them. Both men knew that as surely as they knew their only hope lay in headlong flight. Neither spoke of the possibility that the Apaches attacking their pursuers might only be part of a larger band who might even now be waiting for them somewhere out in the wilderness ahead. Across the long miles to the border it was all Apache land. They kicked the horses into a flat gallop and moved off, heading north.

★　★　★

Through the morning they rode, across mighty stretches of the empty desert, toiling up wide sweeping stretches of broken scrubland, threading their way north, the land beginning to change as they came towards the edge of the desert, the blue-grey peaks of the Huachucas shimmering ahead of them on the horizon. Now they were in a country of little hills and rocky gullies, torn by torrents in the rainy season, scarred by washes and sand-filled riverbeds. Above them the relentless sun shone mercilessly and the featureless land bounced its rays back upwards so that at times they felt as if they were riding through a haze of shimmering heat. They rode with eyes ever alert for movement, the sudden surge of an Apache ambush, pushing hard through the desolate and sterile land, moving upwards now towards the eastern edge of the Huachuca foothills.

Angel glanced at his companions as he rode. Gates leaned forward in the saddle, urging the flagging horse to greater effort. The ponies were flecked now with soapy foam, the punishing pace starting to slow them, their rhythm ragged. Yancey Blantine sat upright in the saddle, his eyes unseeing. The change in the man was enormous. The huge old frame seemed thinner, more brittle, the burning power damped down to a tiny flicker, no more than would sustain life. Only the eyes burned with a never-ending hatred, a consuming need for vengeance. Angel knew that he had been right to give Yancey Blantine no opportunity at any time to free his hands or reach a weapon. If he did, Yancey would go killing-mad and nothing would stop him but death.

He pursed his lips and concentrated upon keeping the horse running. It was still a hell of a long way to Tucson.

★ ★ ★

Fred Little died in the first moments of the charge, a bullet smashing into his forehead and splattering his companions with blood and an oozing grey stuff that slid slimily down the rocks around them. Ronnie Busch took one of the Indians out with a bullet, then another was on him and Busch smashed the Apache down with the butt of his rifle, breaking the wolflike jaw. From a range of two feet he fired his carbine at the Indian, setting the cheap cotton shirt alight. The smell of powdersmoke and burning flesh filled the air and Jerry Kershoe got up to his feet with a very surprised look on his face, two arrows protruding from the nape of his neck. He walked out into the open, his gun dangling in his hand, and one of the Indians ran up and gutted him like a trout, the long knife ending Kershoe's faltering life in an instant. Gregg Blantine shot the Apache in the face as he picked up Kershoe's gun and he heard Busch yell in pain. Wheeling he saw Busch clamping a hand to his thick thigh, which was pumping blood like a tap. Busch sank to the ground in a welter of blood, firing his sixgun as he fell. The Apache who had shot him went over backwards off the top of the rock where he was standing as if he had been snatched off by some invisible hand. Another one jumped up in his place and Gregg shot him in the belly. The Indian grunted and folded forward, falling into the circle of rocks. Busch fell on the kicking body and his arm rose and fell and rose and fell, the Bowie knife thick with blood to its hilt.. Then he fell back, gasping, his whole leg drowning in the pulsing blood from his wound. He tried to lift the sixgun but his hand fell lifeless at his side as the last two Apaches jumped Gregg Blantine, one from the front and the other, Saguarito himself, from the rear. Gregg Blantine roared with sheer anger, glorying at the strength in himself and smashed the Apache in front of him to the ground with a fist like a piece of rock. Saguarito clamped his wiry legs about the huge torso of his enemy, and with a deft and wicked movement planted his long knife into Gregg Blantine's body just below the ribs on the left hand side. Blantine felt the hard, sliding iciness of the blade entering his body and he gave a shriek that froze the Apache clinging to him in horror, for it was not the cry of pain he had expected, it was an exulting, glorying, totally wild cry of madness. He drew back his arm to slide the knife into the huge body again and then Gregg Blantine shook Saguarito off his back as if the Apache had been a small child. The Indian hit the ground and rolled like a cat, coming up crouched with the knife nicely balanced in the palm of his hand and made his move. Saguarito was an Apache, born of this hard land. He had learned how to use a knife from Naiche, whom the Apaches acknowledged their champion knife fighter, and he did everything right, with the killing confidence that came from complete disregard for his own life. His men were all dead and his failure would be a disgrace when he came back to the camp in the Huachucas. All this went through the mind of the Apache as he came at Gregg Blantine, and Gregg Blantine laughed into his black-painted face. His huge hand clamped down on the Apache's forearm and then the free right hand came down in a terrible smashing arc, the clenched fist striking the clamped arm like a hammer. Saguarito's arm broke like a stick and he sagged to his knees with a sick scream. Gregg Blantine let go of the greasy arm and then kicked the Apache with all the strength he had. The stiff, scuffed point of his boot smashed the twisted face into a bloody mask and the Apache went backwards, scrabbling away, the eyes clouded with terror for nothing he had ever seen had been like this insane giant who could not be killed, who felt no pain, whose eyes were like those of the strange ones the Apache found sometimes wandering in the desert. Gregg Blantine stalked after the squirming Apache and then he was upon Saguarito. He caught one of the kicking feet in his right hand, and he twisted it around and over and Saguarito, strong still even in the agony from his broken face and shattered arm, fought helplessly against the inexorable pressure. Gregg Blantine's side was matted with blood but he did not appear to notice it. He twisted and the Apache's body flopped over and then Gregg Blantine had the other foot. He leaned back and swung.

Saguarito screamed once as he came off the ground, full length and held in Gregg Blantine's iron grip. Blantine turned in a short, sharp arc, and smashed the turning body head first against a jagged rock. The Apache's head burst with a sound like a melon hitting a stone floor. Gregg Blantine tossed him aside, and stood there, his huge chest heaving, aware for the first time of the pain in his side. He touched the wound with his left hand and looked in astonishment at the blood on it.

A movement caught his eye. The other Apache who had attacked him was on his feet, and as Gregg watched, he started a headlong run towards the arroyo about thirty feet away. Without haste Gregg Blantine picked up one of the fallen Winchesters and shot the running Apache at the base of the spine. The Indian gave an unearthly shout of agony and fell in a curious broken way, his arms and head thrashing around, eyes clenched tight in a total hell of blinding pain. Gregg Blantine walked across the open sandy space and stood towering above the dying man. He levered the Winchester and fired it straight into the swarthy face, and then he levered the action and fired again and he kept on doing that until the hammer clicked on an empty chamber. Then Gregg Blantine fell, like an old, tall tree coming down in a silent forest, measuring his length upon the boiling sand.

The empty eye of the sun moved dispassionately on.

20

It was Gates' horse that foundered first.

They were labouring up now to the crest of the low foothills of the Huachucas, aiming for a hogback ridge, when the faltering horse went to its knees. Gates, who had been half-expecting it, came off the horse and landed on his feet. The animal lay on its side whickering softly. It would not get up again.

'Kill it,' Angel said.

Gates pulled out his knife and slit the animal's throat in one smooth sweep. The horse's eyes bulged and it started to get up and then it lay down again and it was dead.

'Get up behind Blantine,' Angel said. 'But watch him.'

Blantine said nothing. He did not move as Gates swung up on to the cantle of the saddle behind him and took the reins. Only the hooded eyes moved. If there was anything to see in them, neither of the two men watching Blantine noticed it.

They moved on up to the ridge of the hogback and Angel twisted in the saddle, keen eyes sweeping across the land behind him. The ground fell away from here to the south in smooth-looking gradients, dotted with sagebrush and prickly pear, the tall stalks of ocatillo standing clear against the ochre land, the shimmering malpais below and behind them looking deceptively smooth and featureless from this distance. Ahead of them, the prospect was much the same.

The land sloped steadily down to the north, and they could see the thin white vein of the road to Nogales off on the eastern edge of their sight.

'How far you reckon it is t'Nogales?' Gates asked.

'Not far,' Angel replied. He squinted up at the sun. 'We could be in town by late afternoon. Across the border before nightfall.'

He let his eyes scour the land to the south, behind them, again. In the unseen washes and gullies and river-beds and arroyos that scarred and crisscrossed the broken malpais, an army of Apaches could be hiding and he would not see them. But there had been no dust behind at any time. It didn't figure. If the Apaches had taken all of the pursuers then they would have come after the remaining quarry. If they had been stood off, they would have tried for easier prey. If they had all been killed . . . but that was impossible. For then the pursuers would have taken up the chase again and he would have seen dust. He shook his head. No point in worrying about it. The biggest worry was whether the horses would last until they could get to Nogales and buy fresh ones.

They rode down out of the low hills around Nogales at four in the after-noon. The horses walked with their muzzles down almost touching the ground, the riders slack shouldered in the saddles. As they came nearer the town, Angel's horse blew through its muzzle and its ears came up. It began to pick up its feet. The doubly-laden animal carrying Blantine and Gates also managed to lengthen its gait. They came into the street from the western edge of town, all of them gaunt and coated with the layers of dust that days in the desert had ground into their clothes. Their eyes were deep and burning holes in the chalky faces, and all three had coarse and stubbly chins.

Nogales was a border town, and the three excited little attention. Men came in and men went out of Nogales every hour of the day. Some were honest men, some were thieves, some were lawmen and some were outlaws. Men on the run from the law of the Norteamericanos came to Nogales and received the same shelter and whiskey and women — if they had the price — as Tejanos or Californios cooling their heels while the heat died down in San Antonio or El Paso.

They asked no questions in Nogales. Visitors tended to be wary-eyed and touchy about questions. Visitors always carried guns which they looked ready to use. Nogales fed them, sold them women or whiskey or a bed for the night, then forgot their names and their faces and the direction in which they were travelling.

There were plenty of people in the street, with its adobe houses, its wide shaded ramadas, the larger bulk of a *cantina* here, a store there. On the crowded sidewalks Mexicans in silver-trimmed trousers that flared at the ankle jostled with hard-looking Anglos with sixguns at their waists. Here the mixture of the races met: the swarthy skin of the *mestizo*, the liquid chocolate of the Indians, the handsome bronze of the true Mexican blood, the paler bronze of the Anglos, the Norteameri-canos, all came together in a melting pot of colours and sizes and tongues, American and Spanish and Yaqui and more. Inside one of the *cantinas* they heard a guitar strumming as they rode by, the languid melody of *La Golondrina*.

Angel relaxed gradually, for no one seemed to be paying them the slightest attention. He led the way down the street until he saw a sign swinging on a whitewashed pole by the entrance of an alley alongside a black tarpaper shack with a corrugated iron roof.

'There's a corral,' he said. 'They'll have horses.'

They swung down in the open space before the lean-to that housed the rough stalls for horses. The dust was ankle deep from the passage of many thousands of horses over the years. The animals plunged their muzzles into the trough of water outside the building standing opposite the stalls. From it came the smell of manure and urine, wet straw and the warm stink of horses.

Yancey Blantine pushed the head of his horse aside and plunged his arms into the water, then his face, sluicing the dust and grime of the desert away.

He spluttered with the pleasure of the cooling liquid, standing erect with water pouring off him, his grizzly hair plastered down on his skull.

A man riding past the alleyway looked at the three men standing in the open space, his eyes flicking to Yancey Blantine's face and then the bound wrists. No expression crossed the swarthy features. The man rode on unhurriedly up the street as an old Mexican came out of the stable.

'*Señores*,' he smiled, showing a bright gold tooth. '*Quieren Ustedes alguna cosa?*'

Angel nodded. 'We want three horses,' he said in Spanish.

The old man nodded. His eyes flicked quickly towards Gates' face and then Blantine's. They widened slightly when they touched the bound hands, but that was all. It was not of his concern. His concern was the sale of horses, the care of horses. Nothing more. A man could find enough trouble of his own without sharing anyone else's.

'The *señor* has come to the right establishment,' the old man said. 'At the stable of Juan Solterón only the finest of horses are sold, only the most noble and handsome animals. But of course as the *señor* will appreciate, such animals are of a price befitting the steeds of men like the *señor* and his *caballero* companions.'

'How much?' Angel said abruptly.

The old man frowned. The Norteamericanos had no sense of occasion, no finer feeling for the niceties of bargaining. A man could pass a pleasant hour, two maybe, bargaining over the sale of three horses. A civilized man, of course. A glass of wine, perhaps, from Jerez de la Frontera. A seat in the cool shade of the ramada. And an eloquent discussion of the merits of each individual animal. Such a thing could take up a very pleasant couple of hours. But no, these Americans wanted only to know the price, the price in their all-powerful dollars. He sighed.

'Perhaps when the *señor* has seen the

animals,' he ventured, 'and has had time to realize what a sacrifice it would be for me to part with them, who I have raised from tiny colts to their truly magnificent present state. In the normal way, señores, I would not sell these my very precious animals, but I have had many expenses. A sick child, señores, and a wife who needs special foods, and many visits from the medico. Ah, the times are very bad, señores,' he, sighed, spreading his hands in that gesture universal among merchants of every race. 'I must sacrifice my beautiful horses in the face of the need of my family. I will sell them to you for two hundred dollars American for each horse.'

Angel smiled, and held up a hand as Gates made to step forward, an angry expression on his face.

'Your generosity is truly overwhelming, Don Juan,' he said, using the respectful title and bringing a beaming smile to the old man's face, 'as I am certain that your horses are fine. Alas, my companions and myself must hasten on our journey to the north, where the mother of the old one there is dying of a slow illness. So stricken by grief has he been that we have had to tie his hands so that he will not do himself an injury. It has been our duty, of course, to send much of our money ahead of us to pay for the bills of the doctor, and we can therefore offer something less than you have asked.'

'I understand it well, *señor*,' Solterón said. 'You, too, see my difficulty as I see yours.'

'*Verdad*,' Angel said. 'Which is why I say fifty dollars each horse, not one centavo more.'

Gates ostentatiously touched the butt of his gun and the old man did not miss the gesture. He nodded abruptly, and led the way into the stable, where half a dozen horses stood in stalls along the wall.

'My God!' Gates said. 'He calls these *horses*?'

They were in truth a sorry bunch,

but Angel knew that there would be nothing better anywhere else in Nogales, and if there was they had no time to find them. He unfastened the money belt under his shirt and paid the old man the money for the horses, which they led out into the sunlight.

'I'll get the horses saddled,' he told Gates. 'See if you can round up some supplies. I feel as if I haven't eaten for a week.'

'Why don't we go over to that cantina across the street?' Gates said. 'We could get a bite to eat, mebbe even cut the dust in my throat. Be on our way in half an hour, Frank?'

Angel grinned. He, too, had smelled the mouth-watering odours of chili and beans and frijoles and tortillas coming out of the unprepossessing adobe across the street. Although the sense of urgency he felt inside urged him to head on out of the town now, the look on Gates' face was so comical that he had to relent.

'You like Mex food that much?' he said.

'You better believe it,' Gates said. 'Come on, Frank, we got to eat anyway.'

Gates' final remark clinched it in Angel's mind. Whether they ate out on the open prairie or here in town, they would still have to stop to do it. Eating in town they'd save time in cleaning up, and there would be no campsite to steer any pursuers on to their trail. He wondered again what had happened to Gregg Blantine and the rest of Hurwitch's men.

He told the old man that they would be back soon, and then turned to Yancey Blantine. As he turned, he thought he caught a light of dancing triumph in the old man's eyes, but it was gone even as the thought struck him.

'I'm going to cut your hands loose, Blantine,' he said. 'If you make one false move I'm goin' to shoot your knee apart. You understand?'

Blantine nodded. He hooded his eyes and Angel could not see them.

'I get you,' the old man said. 'Don't worry, I won't try nothin'.'

His voice trembled slightly as if with excitement and Angel frowned.

'What's eating you, Blantine?' he snapped. 'You up to something?'

Blantine shook his head. 'No,' he said hoarsely. He kept his head down and did not meet Angel's eyes. 'Just — just so hungry, I guess. It's been a hard trail we've ridden.'

He chafed his rope-burned wrists, getting the circulation moving, and Angel relaxed, if only to his normal state of wariness.

'Keep your eye on him, too, Pearly,' he said. 'All the time.'

'Sure, sure,' Gates said. 'Where would he run to, anyway?'

He looked across at the cantina again and licked his lips.

'Come on, Frank,' he said.

They started down the alley and then three men stepped into view in the street, guns in their hands.

'Hold it right there!' one of them yelled.

21

They froze in their tracks.

Yancey Blantine let out a great roar of delight.

'Davidson, is that you?' he yelled.

'It's me, Yancey,' replied the tall man in the middle of the trio. 'Step clear while I kill them sonsobitches!'

Angel's eyes quickly took in their predicament. Directly ahead of them and to the right stood the black tarpaper shack with the tin roof. A four foot fence of wooden palings ran from its rear to the horse stalls behind them. The stone horse trough, water trickling from the iron pipe above it, lay in the rectangle formed by the fence and the two buildings. On Gates' left was a low adobe wall, perhaps three feet high. There was no gate in it and it was completely bare and featureless. He let his shoulders rise and then fall. Alone, he might have made a dive for the trough, and then . . . But Gates would be helpless, alone in the middle of the alley with nowhere to run. They would cut him down without mercy.

'Wait on!' Yancey Blantine shouted. 'I want to do this myself!'

He stepped backwards until he was four or five feet behind the two men, and then came around behind Gates. He stretched his hand forward to lift the sixgun out of Gates' holster and as he did Gates moved. He had lifted his arms away from his sides and he was looking down as Yancey Blantine reached forward. His right hand moved like a striking snake and he yanked the man forward, pulling Blantine off balance and whirling him around into the centre of the alley, all arms and legs like a runaway windmill, Yancey Blantine shouting in sudden panic as his balance went. And in that same moment Gates was moving, his long legs driving for the wall, vaulting over it even as Angel threw himself down and rolled off to the right behind the stone trough, his gun already in his hand, blasting the first man off his feet down at the entrance to the alley, the other two throwing shots at Gates, who was already over the wall and on its sheltered far side, poking his gun over the top and firing at the two men in the street. They had run behind a boxlike adobe that stood about ten or fifteen feet down the street on the left of the entrance, and they pounded around it, heading for the adobe wall which ran at right angles to the one behind which Gates was sheltering. Angel got quickly to his feet and ran across the alley. Yancey Blantine lay rigid on the ground, his eyes wide with terror as the two behind the adobe fired hasty shots at Gates. The big man came up and vaulted over the wall and down on their side.

'You move and I'll kill you sure!' rasped Angel to the old man. Blantine nodded. He buried his head in his arms and lay still as Angel scuttled over to the wall. Shots whined off the top of the wall as the two men in the open space between the adobe and the next building pinned them down with seeking fire.

Gates, crouched low, ran along the adobe wall and made it to the gate pulled back off the street, thrusting fresh cartridges into his sixgun as he knelt in the dust. Then he pumped his arm up and down as a signal to Angel and ran straight out into the wide dusty street at an angle, quartering across the empty space like a banderillero running to meet and yet avoid the charging bull. The two men in the yard of the adobe building were crouched at the foot of the wall, and they felt rather than heard or saw Gates out there. They whirled around, coming to their feet with their guns blazing as Gates dropped one of them and rolled forward in the dust, trying for the shelter of the angle made by the next building. The tall one that Yancey Blantine had called Davidson stood up, and held his sixgun in both hands, sighting it carefully. Angel shot him in the back of the head and the tall man went down flat dead in the dirt with his face blown away. Angel got up and turned around to see Yancey Blantine standing behind him with a Winchester carbine in his hands, the hammer eared back.

'Tell your friend Gates to throw his gun down an' get over here!' snarled Blantine. 'An' let go o' that sixgun while you're at it!'

Angel stood for a long second and looked at Blantine, who made a nervous gesture with the carbine.

'Do it!' he said.

'Pearly!' yelled Angel. 'Blantine's got the drop on me!'

He watched as Gates got up from the dusty street, slapping at his clothes with his hands. Gates made an elaborate show of tossing his sixgun away wide of where he was standing and started to walk towards them and Angel cursed himself for his own stupidity. He had let Blantine fool him beautifully with that act of being terrified. Then while he and Gates had been occupied with the gunmen in the street, Blantine had scuttled back up the alley to the horses and lifted one of the carbines out of the saddle. That easy. He shook his head in self-disgust.

Gates came up on the far side of the wall.

'You never give up, do you, Blantine?' he said quietly.

'Get over on this side o' that wall where I can see you!' snarled Blantine. He made a vicious gesture with the carbine.

Gates shrugged, as though humouring a small boy, and vaulted lithely over the low adobe wall, standing with his hands on his hips watching the wary renegade. There was a real change in Yancey Blantine. The eagle look of power was back in the mad old eyes, and the big frame was erect again, the shoulders straight and proud. The gun in his hand made all the difference. He had known the chance would come and when it had come he had taken it.

'Over there,' he said. 'Behind the stable!'

'You goin' to shoot us now, Blantine?' Gates asked mildly.

'*Right* now!' snapped Blantine. 'Move!'

He stepped back and gestured again with the gunbarrel. They had to walk past him towards the stable and Yancey Blantine took no chances on either of them coming close enough to jump him.

Gates turned and started down the alley, passing Blantine at the same time that Angel came up on his right and neither of them saw Angel move. A long time ago, when he had first started to work for the Department of Justice, Angel had spent three or four hours with the Armourer in the echoing basement on the Tenth Street side of the Justice Department building. After their talk, the Armourer had fashioned a special belt for Angel, with a clip buckle that became a razor-edged knife, a length of two feet of piano wire stitched to the inside of it which when unfastened became a garrotting wire. He had also spent some time on Angel's boots. On the right hand side of the right boot and the left hand side of the left boot, between the soft inner leather and the tougher outer, he had sewn a channel, its opening concealed by the pull loops; and into that channel on each side he had fitted a flat handled, flat bladed throwing knife, perfectly balanced and made from the finest Solingen steel.

It was one of these knives that whickered past Gates' chin as Angel moved, too fast for Gates to know what he was doing, not quite fast enough to prevent Yancey Blantine yanking on the trigger as he felt the danger without ever seeing it. The bullet burned a bright red welt down the length of Angel's outflung arm from the wrist to the elbow and he cursed as the pain seared him, the sound of his oath lost in the screech of pain as the unerringly thrown Solingen knife turned once gently, slowly, winking in the sunlight as it drove right through Yancey Blantine's upper arm, shearing the bicep and making the old man drop the carbine as if it had suddenly become a dead-weight of a ton. Yancey Blantine's left arm dropped like a wet rag at his side and he stared in disbelief at the rubber-hilted knife lodged in the bloody mess of his arm.

He was still staring at it when Gates hit him.

The big man hit Yancey Blantine with the cold precision of a butcher taking an axe to a side of beef and the sound his fist made when it hit the old man's jaw was almost the same. Blantine's knees folded and he went down into the dirt. Angel went over to the horse-trough and plunged his arm into the water. It turned faintly pink, then pinker, the blood spiralling and coiling in the clear water like some red and eerie snake.

'All right?' Gates said. He had pulled the knife out of Yancey Blantine's arm and was staring at it. He shook his head, then stuck it in the dirt while he ripped the sleeve from Blantine's shirt and bound it tightly around the wounded arm.

'He'll never use that arm again,' he said.

'He wouldn't have been needing it long anyway,' Angel replied coldly. 'He'll hang in Tucson.'

Gates finished his bandaging and then dragged the old man across the alley into one of the open stalls. He laid the wounded arm gently in front of Yancey Blantine, and bound the other firmly and tightly to the thick wooden upright of stall. Then he found another length of rope and bound Blantine's feet. He stood up.

Angel had washed the throwing knife and was stowing it away in the scabbard on the side of his boot.

'That's some place to keep a knife,' Gates said. 'If you got a fork on the other side, we could go eat.'

They walked together down the alley as the people of Nogales came slowly out of doors once more, grouping around the dead men in the street, and watching the two men crossing the street towards the cantina as though they were supernatural.

22

They crossed the border the next morning.

While they were in the *cantina* an elderly man in the conservative grey of a Spanish businessman had come up to them at their table. With him were two armed men who carried rifles.

'*Señores,*' the old man said, 'I am Don Ricardo Bicaforto, the *alcalde* of Nogales. Those men are my *alguacils* — how do you say, my sheriffs.'

Angel nodded. He pushed his empty plate away and Gates followed suit.

They had eaten enough for any four men.

'This fracas in the street,' the *alcalde* said. 'I am afraid I must ask you to accompany me.'

'We fought in self-defence,' Angel said. 'I am sure that many saw it.'

'Doubtless, *señor,*' Bicaforto said,

'but even so . . . ' He spread his hands and one of the two *alguacils* shifted his weight on his feet and moved the rifle slightly.

'You will permit me?' Angel said, gesturing towards his belt.

'Of course,' the *alcalde* said. 'But carefully, *señor*. My men are good men, and they will kill you if you make them.'

Angel reached for a pocket inside his belt and brought something out which he laid on the table. It caught the sunlight and glittered dully. The *alcalde* said something beneath his breath and picked it up. His eyes flickered over the screaming eagle, the circular seal, and his lips moved as he read the words: 'Department of Justice, United States of America.' He looked up.

'You are of the Department of Justice of America?' he said. Angel nodded and heard Gates mutter, 'Well, I'll be damned!'

'I have a prisoner who I am taking back to Tucson for trial,' Angel said quietly to the old man. 'His name is

Yancey Blantine.'

Bicaforto's eyes narrowed and he hissed through his teeth.

'Blantine?' he said. 'I have heard of that one.'

'He's going to hang,' Angel told him flatly. 'He burned a town in Arizona, killed a lot of men and women up there.'

'Yes, I have heard this, too,' the *alcalde* said. 'But the law of the United States does not extend into Mexico, *señor*.'

'I know it,' Angel said. He left the words hanging there and the old man smiled.

'However, if you truly have Yancey Blantine a prisoner . . . ?' he said.

'We have him,' Angel said.

'Then what you do serves Mexico also, *señor*, and I would be a fool to stand in your way. May I ask your name?'

'Frank Angel,' was the reply.

'Angel,' said the alcalde, smiling. '*Angel custodio, tal bez?*'

'In this instance, yes,' Angel returned the smile. 'Guardian angel is right.'

The old man nodded and gave a signal to his two sheriffs who stepped back and lowered their guns.

'Is there some way in which I can assist you?' he said.

They had told him that they needed horses, and horses were provided, good horses, sound of wind and with plenty of bottom. They were given food for their journey, and water in canteens. Don Ricardo had seen to it that they had ammunition, and that comfortable beds were made up for them in the rooms above the *juzgado*. Yancey Blantine was lodged below them in the jail under the baleful gaze of the *alguacils*.

Next morning they were on their way, the '*Vaya con Dios!*' of Don Ricardo still ringing in their ears. They passed the stone cairn that marked the line of the border and rode through the golden morning up along the valley of the Santa Cruz, Keystone Peak rearing six thousand feet ahead of them in the sunshine.

'We should be at Arivaca by noon,' Angel said. 'With luck we'll be in tucson tonight.'

'That's a thought,' Gates said, smiling. 'No, Blantine?'

Yancey Blantine scowled and said nothing. The golden morning meant less than nothing to him. Everything was gone. His sons were dead, his power shattered once and for all by this saturnine man on the horse alongside him. The *alguacils* at Nogales had enjoyed telling him who Angel was, and there had been an awful finality about the words 'Department of Justice.'

'You aiming to go back to Colorado?' Angel asked Gates.

'Not for me,' Gates grinned. 'I been there. Thought I might try San Francisco. I never been there.'

'You got five thousand dollars reward coming,' Angel reminded him. 'You could buy a spread with that kind of money.'

Gates nodded, his face sobering for a moment.

'I got to go to Abilene first,' he said.

'The buttermilk and honey girl?'

'Ahuh,' Gates agreed. 'Might be she'd want to hear about Chris.'

'Could be,' Angel said. 'The thought's a good one, anyway.'

They crested a ridge and saw the little town of Arivaca below them by the river. They pushed the horses on down the hill.

23

Gregg Blantine got to Nogales more dead than alive.

He found a doctor on a narrow street running at right angles to the main plaza and told the man to patch up his wound. When the man hesitated, Gregg Blantine stuck his sixgun under the doctor's nose and told him that he would kill him if he did not. The doctor was an eminently sensible man and did exactly what he was told. When he had seen the wound in Gregg Blantine's side he knew it did not make any difference what he did.

While the doctor dressed the wound with deft fingers Blantine lapsed into near unconsciousness. He had killed three horses getting to Nogales, and only the enormous reserves of strength in his giant body had kept him going — that and his single-minded, almost insane determination to catch up with the man called Angel. In the madness of his fixed idea, it never once occurred to Gregg Blantine that he had never seen Angel, would not know the man on sight. Something inside him told him he would know Angel when the time came. And then he would kill him.

Later the doctor brought him coffee, laced with tequila, and Blantine sat up. His wound was firmly bound with fresh bandages that smelled of antiseptic. He felt much better and said so.

'*Sí, señor*, of course,' the doctor said. 'But you must go with much care, very much care.'

'I got to find a man called George Davidson,' Blantine said. 'You know him?'

'Davidson?' The doctor's voice was nervous, tentative. 'He was a friend of yours?'

The words bounced in Gregg Blantine's head, as though they were echoing. 'Was?' he snapped. 'You sayin' he's dead?'

The doctor nodded unhappily. 'Alas,

yes, *señor*. He was killed but last night in a fracas, in the town, two others with him.'

He told Gregg Blantine about the fight that had happened, the news of which was now all over the town, gory details being added at each retelling. He told Gregg Blantine about the miserable old man who had spent the night in the *juzgado*; laughing, never knowing how close at that moment he was to violent death as Blantine forced himself to hear it all, his huge hands clenching and unclenching in his lap. Finally he heard what he wanted to know: that they had left town that morning, heading north for Tucson. There was only one way they could go: up the valley of the Santa Cruz, through Arivaca and past the San Xavier del Bac mission and into Tucson from the south. He got up, reeling slightly. His head was light, and faint stars swam behind the retina of his eyes.

The Mexican doctor put a hand under the big man's elbow, steadying him. '*Señor*,' he said, in alarm, 'are you all right?'

Gregg Blantine nodded. 'I'm all right,' he said. He shook off the helpful hand. 'I'm all right, I said!'

The doctor ducked his head and said no more. There was no point in telling this one to look after his wound, to avoid exertion, not to ride, not to lift. There was the look in those eyes, the tension in the giant frame, the way the huge hands curled and unclenched all providing him with direct evidence that nothing he said would be heard. He was a good doctor, by his lights, and he regretted stupidity. But this great giant of a man would kill himself no matter what he was told.

Gregg Blantine went down the street to the stable and bought a horse. He hardly looked at the animal, although he got a good one because the man who sold it to him was too frightened to do anything else. It didn't matter to Gregg Blantine. He knew he was going to kill the animal anyway.

24

They rode into Arivaca just after noon.

There was nothing much special about the place, just another sleepy little Arizona town scattered along both sides of one street. A general store here, a hardware store there, a livery stable with a smithy next to it, and at the Tucson end of town a false fronted frame building with the legend 'The Oasis: H. Poirot, Prop.'.

'I wouldn't mind a dust cutter, Frank,' Gates said, easing his body in the saddle. 'How about you?'

Angel nodded. 'Not a bad idea,' he said. He stood back while Gates helped Yancey Blantine down out of the saddle. Since their experience in the alleyway in Nogales, they had taken no chances at all with the old man, who had reverted again to the sullen silence which characterised him throughout the major part of their flight from Agua Caliente and all the way to the border. They both knew now, though, that the agile brain never stopped figuring and planning, running this way and that like a rat in a maze, gnawing at the problem until it saw a solution and when it saw the solution — Well, they didn't plan on providing Yancey Blantine with any solutions between here and Tucson.

They pushed into the saloon and sat Yancey Blantine down at one of the tables. Gates went to the bar and ordered beer, while Angel sat opposite the old renegade. Blantine spat on the sawdusted floor.

There was no one in the place, unless you counted a drunken cowboy with his head in his arms, asleep at one of the tables in the rear. Two girls were drinking beer at the end of the bar. They started over to the table but Gates stopped them and said something. They looked at Angel and the prisoner and shrugged, going back to their stools. The bartender opened his newspaper and started reading it.

'Maybe we should get some steak an' eggs,' Gates said. 'I got a lot of eatin' to catch up on.'

'I'd as soon push on,' Angel said. 'We can eat in Tucson. I'll buy you the best dinner the Scat Fly can cook!'

'That'd be — '

Whatever Gates had been going to say was lost in the terrible booming crash of a shotgun that blasted the windows of the saloon into shivering, whirring shards of broken glass whose sound blended with the whickering purr of the slugs. Gates was snatched out of his chair as the far wall erupted in splinters of plaster and wood, a picture clattering to the floor. Angel was already going sideways out of the chair, dragging Blantine down to the floor with him, the sixgun in Angel's hand bucking against his palm as he threw two shots at the looming shape outside the saloon.

One of the girls screamed, a short sharp terrified sound, as Gates tried to get up from where he had fallen, going around in a half circle on the floor that was slick with his blood.

Angel slid across the floor and tipped a table forward, moving to the assistance of his fallen friend as the doors swung open and he saw the muzzle of the shotgun poke into the room. Again the twin barrels erupted with smoke and flame and he heard the heavy gauge slugs smash into the table, tearing great chunks of wood out of it which flickered past his face. He felt blood trickling down his cheek.

'Pa!' he heard a broken voice shout. 'Pa! You in there, Pa?'

He saw Yancey Blantine scuttle around behind the table where they had been sitting. His face was alight with savage joy.

'Gregg!' Yancey Blantine yelled. 'In here, boy! You got one o' them!'

Yancey Blantine edged towards the shattered window and shouted hoarsely, 'Throw me a gun, boy! A gun, a gun!'

Angel threw a shot at the old man,

more meant to keep him out of the fight than to hit him, and his slug smashed shards of the broken window in a shower over Yancey Blantine's head. The old man ducked down as a sixgun was lobbed in through the window, landing with an iron *clunk!* within a few feet of the old renegade's reaching left hand. Angel fired without sighting and his slug smashed the sixgun spinning across the floor, whipping it away from the reach of the old man.

'Where is he, Pa?' he heard Gregg Blantine yell. There were sounds out in the street, the sounds of other men shouting, feet stamping along the board sidewalks.

'Right opposite the door, boy,' shouted Yancey Blantine. 'Behind the table!'

Angel saw the batwings part again and he was on his feet as the barrel of the shotgun poked into the room, moving as fast as he knew how across the floor of the saloon. The shotgun went off again with an enormous sound that flattened his eardrums, and then he grasped it in both hands and heaved Gregg Blantine into the saloon. The big man came in on the run, catching his balance as he ran and Angel stepped forward and with every ounce of strength he could muster, slammed the barrel of his gun down on the bony point directly behind Gregg Blantine's left ear. The terrible force of the blow drove the giant to his knees, but it did not knock him out. He shook his head, trying to clear it, as Angel stepped closer to him and raised the sixgun for another blow. This time Gregg Blantine whirled on his knees and caught Angel around the waist. His huge arms clamped around his quarry like the paws of a grizzly, and Angel felt the breath rush out of his lungs as Gregg Blantine lifted him off his feet. He pounded the gunbutt into the giant's face, grinding, murderous, punishing, breaking blows that smeared Gregg's nose into a broken pulp, splitting the brows, the whole mad face dissolving into a bloody, macabre mask of torn flesh and bone, and still Gregg Blantine raised Angel higher, roaring in agony and rage, up until Angel was level with Gregg Blantine's chest. Then with one surging sweep, Gregg Blantine threw Angel against the bar. Angel's back hit the bar and the wave of pain that shocked through him made him black out. He fell forward on to the sawdusted floor, his head spinning, every muscle in his body paralysed and incapable of obeying the frantic signals his brain was sending to them. Gregg Blantine lurched over to where Angel lay on the floor and raised his foot, putting the weight of his whole body behind the kick that landed in the small of Angel's back. Angel's body lifted a foot off the ground and he lay huddled in the corner, fighting to breathe, sucking air desperately into lungs which felt as though they had turned to stone. He lay there with his eyes open as Gregg Blantine bent down and picked up the shotgun. Yancey Blantine came out from his hiding place behind the over-turned table and watched as Gregg poked a shell into each of the two barrels. The giant snapped the gate closed and pointed the gun at Angel.

None of them had seen Gates get up.

He came across the room half crouched, his shoulder down, and the force of his charge swept Gregg Blantine against the wall. The shotgun exploded into the air, smashing huge chunks of wood and plaster from the ceiling, breaking one of the oil lamps into a thousand flying fragments. Fighting for every breath, Angel tried to rise. He saw, but could hardly believe that he saw the strong, solid body of Pearly Gates, spattered with the multiple marks of shotgun slugs, blood dappling his body with a strange pattern of bright reds and darker browns, throw a strong forearm around Gregg Blantine's neck from behind, then clamp his left hand upon the wrist of the arms around the giant's neck.

Angel saw Blantine's eyes start from his head. He whirled around, trying to fight Gates off his back, but Gates hung on. His teeth were set deep into the lower lip and Angel could see it was bitten clean through in Gates' agony, but Gregg Blantine could not shake off the man on his back, and Gates kept on increasing the terrible pressure on Blantine's throat. Blantine's tongue protruded and he made an awful, choking, retching sound, his arms thrashing behind him, turning and bashing against the wall, hurling himself in blind and unreasoning terror around the room to dislodge the terrible killing thing on his back. For the first time, Angel got a full breath into his lungs and tried to move his feet, trying for a handhold on the bar as Gregg Blantine blundered back again into the wall of the saloon, the glasses and bottles behind the bar jingling and tinkling with the weight of the impact.

Angel saw now too that there was bright red blood staining Gregg Blantine's middle, and as he watched the bright stain became a pumping spurt, as though something had broken open inside the man. Gregg Blantine went down to his knees and Gates went with him. Gates' eyes were completely closed now, and his legs scrabbled for a moment on the floor before they found the purchase they needed. Angel saw the arm muscles tighten even more and Gregg Blantine's eyes went up into his head. Then Yancey Blantine stepped forward and emptied his sixgun into Pearly Gates' back. It was done so suddenly that Angel had no chance to prevent it, and he saw the old man start back as Gates' shirt flickered briefly into a flame which quickly died, smouldering, acrid smoke rising from the blackened bloody pit in the big man's back. Gates at last slipped from Gregg Blantine's back, and Blantine turned around to look at his father, his hands reaching for the old man, and started forward. Angel saw that the bullets which Yancey Blantine had fired at such terribly short range into Pearly

Gates' back had gone right through the big man and smashed Gregg Blantine's spine. Gregg Blantine fell at his father's feet and then Yancey Blantine saw what he had done and finally went completely insane.

25

'You say neither of them had relatives, dependants?' the Attorney-General asked. Angel shook his head.

'It . . . I wish there were something I could do,' the older man said.

'There's nothing,' Angel told him. 'I did all there was.' It was a fortnight later, and it was all over.

Angel had brought old Yancey Blantine to Tucson, a dribbling, haunted, insane wreck of a man who screamed throughout the night and wept uncontrollably through the day. There was no trial. The United States Marshal had sent a deputy with Yancey Blantine to Yuma Penitentiary. They would do what they could for him there, but the doctors who had examined him in Tucson did not think he would live long. The power of the renegade Blantines was utterly broken along the border anyway. Not a man but moved in that dangerous wilderness had not heard of the things that had happened in the Santa Eulalia country and the word was out: the Blantines are finished.

'They were good men, Frank,' the Attorney-General said softly. 'I'm sure it was how they would have wanted it to be.'

'They wanted it to be fun,' Angel said bitterly, 'Fun! They were going down there for a jaunt, a diversion. Then they were coming back, Chris to his girl in Abilene, Gates — ah, the hell with it!'

He got up and walked across the room, staring out of the window at the people on Pennsylvania Avenue. What the hell did they care about two good men dead? What did they care about the men who kept their laws? Not a damned thing. They ate and slept and fornicated and quarrelled and competed and lived and died and never cared.

'You're due some leave,' the Attorney-General said quietly.

'I know it,' Angel said. 'I thought I might go up to New York for a few days.'

'Good idea,' enthused the Attorney-General, leaning back in his chair. He took one of the black cigars and lit it, smiling as it wreathed his face in thick blue smoke.

'Miss Rowe around?' Angel asked casually.

'Why, no,' the older man replied, just as casually. 'Why do you ask?'

'I thought I might take her to dinner.'

'Oh, what a pity,' the Attorney-General said. 'She just went off on a two week vacation. I thought she was looking a little peaked, so I told her to get some sunshine. Sent her to stay with some friends of mine.'

Angel's face brightened. 'Where would that be?' he asked.

'Arizona,' the older man replied imperturbably, and then laughed out loud at the look on the face of his Special Investigator. 'Tucson, to be exact.'

'Well, I'll be a sad sonofabitch!' Angel

said. 'I just came from there!'

'Now, Frank,' said the Attorney-General. 'Good secretaries are hard to find in this town. Call it a safety precaution, if you like. I watched her the last time you were here.' He shook his head. 'Sorry.'

'You did it on purpose,' Angel said. There was a slow smile coming into his eyes, and it gladdened the man in the big chair behind the desk. Angel was young, and very good. He did not want to lose him, and he knew how hard the death of his friends had hit Angel.

He nodded. 'I'm afraid I did.'

Angel walked to the door.

'There'll be other times,' he said.

'Have a good time in New York,' the Attorney-General said.

'Go to hell,' Angel replied and slammed the door. The man behind the desk smiled. He'd been told to go to hell before.

We do hope that you have enjoyed reading this large print book.

Did you know that all of our titles are available for purchase?

We publish a wide range of high quality large print books including:
Romances, Mysteries, Classics
General Fiction
Non Fiction and Westerns

Special interest titles available in large print are:
The Little Oxford Dictionary
Music Book, Song Book
Hymn Book, Service Book

Also available from us courtesy of Oxford University Press:
Young Readers' Dictionary
(large print edition)
Young Readers' Thesaurus
(large print edition)

For further information or a free brochure, please contact us at:
Ulverscroft Large Print Books Ltd.,
The Green, Bradgate Road, Anstey,
Leicester, LE7 7FU, England.
Tel: (00 44) **0116 236 4325**
Fax: (00 44) **0116 234 0205**

Other titles in the
Linford Western Library:

NEVADA HAWK

Hank J. Kirby

The long trail ended at Castle Rock in New Mexico Territory. Nevada found the man who had murdered his wife — then killed him as he'd planned. What was the next step now? A talented gunman like Nevada was always in demand. He didn't care what type of work he took on, or how dangerous. Life — his own, that is — no longer mattered much any more. Or did it . . . ? He would breathe plenty of gunsmoke before he found the answer.

BRIGHAM'S WAY

Richard Wyler

Brigham, Seth and Jacob Tyler came to the Colorado badlands in search of gold. They found it alright — but they also found it took a deal of holding onto. There were violent killers ready to take it from them . . . and the three brothers would have to match bullet for bullet for each of them to retain his wealth, and forge his own way in life.

BRIGAND'S BLADE

David Bingley

Mike Liddell is a trouble-shooter for the wealthy Beauclerc family. His former partner was Roxy Barlow. After a time, a man with designs on the Beauclerc fortune exploits Roxy's weakness in liquor to gain a footing in the Beauclerc home. Roxy causes Mike some real problems — but helps fight the opposition. Madame la Baronne de Beauclerc narrowly avoids a disastrous marriage, and Mike is almost cremated before the smoke fades, in a violent and deadly showdown.

DEAD WHERE YOU STAND!

Tyler Hatch

Russ Conrad was a good man, tired of riding the rough edges of life, and Longbow Basin seemed a good place to settle. However, Fergus Keefer with his giant Slash K ranch was greedy for land, and wouldn't give a small rancher a chance — his hardcases saw to that. Guns and fists escalated to brushfires and murder. Now Conrad would have to fight for the peace and quiet he sought — but fighting was something he knew plenty about . . .

TWO-GUN TROUBLE

Gillian F. Taylor

Heads turn when Jonah Durrell rides into Motherlode. A handsome, charming man, he is also a successful manhunter, as good with his fists as with his guns. Jonah just wants to enjoy himself at Miss Jenny's parlour-house; however, his visit is interrupted by the brutal murder of one of the girls. Someone wants Miss Jenny out of town — but she won't be pushed around. And Jonah will always help a damsel in distress. But at what cost?